The Land of Yesterday

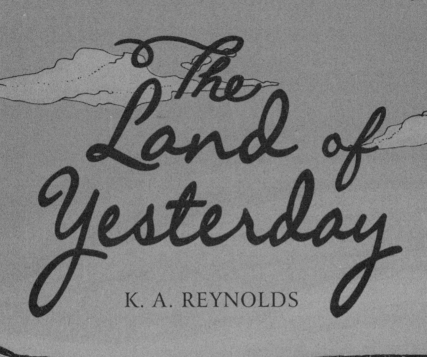

The Land of Yesterday

K. A. REYNOLDS

HARPER
An Imprint of HarperCollins*Publishers*

DEDICATION

For my mother, to whom I threw the letter, and for my grandmother, who caught it. You are the light and the love and the daisies. Every story leads back to you.

(And for the one reading this now, who may need a friend to help navigate the darkness, listen close. I've traveled this dark path before and know where the lanterns are hidden. It's treacherous to go alone. But if you're ready, take my hand. We can walk together.

I'll tell you a story along the way. . . .)

COURAGE, DEAR HEART.

—C. S. LEWIS

Chapter 1

THE TUESDAY CECELIA THOUGHT TUESDAYS
COULDN'T GET ANY WORSE

Six weeks plus one day ago, Cecelia Dahl understood the world. She resided in a town called Hungrig, in a crooked house named Widdendream. Daisies circled the lake outside her window. Sharp mountains loomed over her town. Cecelia's midnight-blue hair grew long, fast, and cantankerous. Dogs barked. Cats meowed. Widdendream cared for its residents, as all good houses should. And Cecelia's family loved her, unconditionally.

Then Monday rolled into Tuesday and Cecelia did the bad thing. Now the world had narrowed down to this: Tuesday hated Cecelia and Cecelia hated it back.

It being another evil Tuesday, Cecelia didn't want to go to school. But today being evil, what she wanted didn't matter.

Upon first inspection, her classroom appeared nonthreatening. Same faces, same teacher, same desk. Still, she had to keep reminding herself that even ax murderers looked pleasant enough with their axes behind their backs.

To distract herself, Cecelia made sketches with her special pen. She drew daisies, and an interstellar hot-air balloon exploring unknown lands. She sneaked peeks at her favorite adventure book, *Around the World in Eighty Minutes*, while Miss Podsnappery assured the class that the Gnomes of the Stratosphere of Now most certainly did not exist.

In Cecelia's opinion, people who didn't believe in fantastical things were awfully hard to listen to.

"Cecelia?" Miss Podsnappery pushed up her horn-rimmed glasses and sidled over to Cecelia's desk. "Whatever do you call that instrument in your hand?"

Every eye in class turned to Cecelia. They judged her charcoal sweater, black-and-gray-striped dress, frayed tights, and scuffed boots before moving on to her unique fountain pen. It had a barrel of gold and glass made to resemble a map of the stars. Its cap was carved like the gears of a clock and screwed on tight. The inner lapis-blue ink cartridge even came with a special plug to keep the ink inside, and there was not another like it in all the world. Usually, Cecelia left her pen at home, but today, she felt she might need it.

"This," Cecelia replied, holding up the device in question, "is what is called a *pen*." Miss Podsnappery was a kind yet simple creature and quite easily confused, so Cecelia tried to keep her answers as straightforward as possible.

"A *pen* you say?" Miss Podsnappery grinned, displaying two rows of skewed yellow teeth. "Imagine!" She unhunched herself from over Cecelia's desk and turned to the class. "Isn't that wonderful?"

The class replied with silence, the language of tumbleweeds and gape-mouth stares.

"Yes," Cecelia said with a sigh. "Though it's no *ordinary* pen. My mother gave it to me last year. She claimed it could perform miracles, ones that brought the writer and reader together, like magic." Cecelia lowered her eyes and wrapped her hair around her neck like a scarf. "Once, I even believed it powerful enough to reach those who'd passed into the Land of Yesterday. Now I'm not so sure."

"Ah." Miss Podsnappery nodded, eyebrows crumpled into squiggly lines. "I understand completely."

But Cecelia knew Miss Podsnappery didn't understand what she was talking about. Like many adults, her teacher's imagination had shrunk considerably since childhood. Had

Cecelia told Miss Podsnappery about the letters she'd tried sending to Yesterday, or the awful thing she'd done to prompt them, her teacher's brain might have exploded. Cecelia would not take that chance. She had hurt enough people already.

Without warning, Miss Podsnappery's birdlike head jerked toward the door. A hush fell over the class. Distant footsteps drew closer outside in the hall. Miss Podsnappery gulped. "Principal Furbelow."

It was a well-known fact that their principal detested leaving his office for any reason other than a student emergency or full-blown calamity. It being evil Tuesday, Cecelia stared down at her fidgeting hands, certain of only one thing.

Something terrible was coming.

And it was coming for her.

Cecelia squeezed her special pen tighter. As she did, memories of her mother flooded her mind. Of strolling to the lake holding hands as the wind played toss with their hair. Of sharing stories by the water's edge, surrounded by daisies. Cecelia could almost hear their laughter now. Once, she had known how to make her mother smile.

Not anymore.

Principal Furbelow's footfalls hit the hall like thunderclaps shouting Cecelia's name.

CE—CE—LIA—DAHL.

CE—CE—LIA—DAHL.

The desks shook. The window glass trembled. The skies darkened to hurricane gray. Principal Furbelow knocked on the door.

Thud.

Thud.

THUD.

And Miss Podsnappery let him in.

Every child followed the principal with a pointed gaze. He stopped at Cecelia's desk, as she knew he would, and stared down at her. Her skin crawled with terror. She wanted to run and hide. But evil Tuesday had her trapped. When the principal opened his mouth to speak, Cecelia braced herself.

"????? ????, ???'?? ???? ?? ???? ???? ??." A series of groans and grunts and alien sounds she didn't understand was all she heard when he spoke.

Cecelia turned in confusion and asked Penelope Ness, who sat in the desk behind her, "Could you understand what he said?" But all that came out of Penelope's mouth were honks and coughs and nonsense, a foreign language of farts.

Cecelia swung around to Bram Popinjay—a friend with fabulous hair and crooked teeth. Bram enjoyed Cecelia's strangeness, unlike most everyone else. "Bram, can you understand me?" She pointed at the principal. "Can you understand him?"

Bram shook his head sadly and answered, "?'?? ??????

????????? ???. ??? ??? ????? ??? ???? ???? ??????."

Word farts.

Oh souls.

She'd read about this phenomenon, technically known as "Wordfartopotamus Syndrome," in *Fantastical Maladies Weekly*. Some experts didn't believe in the syndrome. Those who did claimed the ailment came and went without warning, and affected only those who'd lost loved ones to Yesterday. The article said individuals caught under its spell experienced a language breakdown so severe, anyone they encountered who had never lost a loved one sounded identical to trumpeting farts. But why would she get this now, and not six weeks earlier when she'd lost her brother?

Unless Yesterday had taken another someone she loved.

Cecelia, still looking helplessly at Bram, spun around so fast at the thought, her hair swept her desk and knocked her neatly organized pencils and perfectly stacked papers to the floor. She glanced at the mess and gasped. Her chin trembled. Heat prickled her eyes and Cecelia burst into tears, right in the middle of class.

Six weeks and one day earlier, random outbreaks of Wordfartopotamus Syndrome and messes of pencils and papers wouldn't have bothered her a bit. But now everything brought panic and fear.

When Principal Furbelow motioned for her to stand, Cecelia grabbed her things, and gripped her special pen tight. She thought of her mother, who shared her midnight-blue hair, bronze skin, and odd arrangement of freckles. Not long ago, they shared most things, except for ice-cream cones, toothpicks, the way they hung the toilet-paper roll, and, lastly, their eyes. Cecelia's were as midnight blue as her hair, yet her mother's were bluish purple, the same shade as her name, Mazarine. Icy slime pulsed through Cecelia's veins as Principal Furbelow led Cecelia from class.

Descending the second-floor staircase, Cecelia's footsteps echoed into infinity. Each clunk knocked on a door to her memories. Cecelia recalled the time her mother took her little brother to the lake instead of her. How Celadon had even returned with daisies in his hair. "Why did you take him and not me?" Cecelia asked, hurt. "Daisies by the lake are our special thing."

Her mother held her closer and smiled. "I have a story for you. Did you know that on the day of your birth, you left a piece of your heart inside me?" Cecelia shook her head, eyes wide. "It's true. A strand of your unique you-ness wound out from your heart and rooted into mine like a seed. Soon after, that thread of Cecelianess bloomed into a daisy, and filled me with the most glorious light. I shone so brightly,

7

another seed took root, and soon, it blossomed into a daisy right beside yours."

Cecelia glared, and groaned, "Celadon."

The corners of Mazarine's eyes crinkled like tiny bird feet. "You should feel proud, Cecelia. That second bloom could have sprung up anywhere, but chose to be by your side, to always look up to you." Cecelia rested her head on her mother's chest, listening for the flowers in her heart. And as she drifted off to sleep, her mother whispered warmly in Cecelia's ear, "Daisies will always remind me of you. . . ."

With a few parting honks and gassy declarations, Principal Furbelow escorted Cecelia outside onto the front steps. He nodded to someone in the distance, patted her shoulder, and then left Cecelia to her fate.

Fog rolled through the parking lot toward her. It didn't take long for a familiar form to slog out of the mist. Mussed black hair, smudges of dirt on his face, eggplant-colored suit, buttoned and hung all wrong.

Father.

Aubergine Dahl shuffled up the school steps toward Cecelia. He stared at her as if searching for something to say—something he couldn't find. Yet, despite the panic lighting fireworks in her veins, Cecelia rushed him with open arms, and squeezed.

He smelled of misery, musty basements, and home.

"What's happened?" Cecelia grabbed his filthy lapels. He continued to stare at her blankly, with eyes so like her brother Celadon's, pale green as shallow seas. "Why are you here early? Say something. Anything to let me know you and Mother are okay."

Her father pushed a stray bit of hair out of Cecelia's eye and gave her a sad smile. "I've been better. But I'll live. I'll tell you the rest in the c—"

"Oh my souls!" Cecelia screeched so loud, blackbirds propelled from the trees. "You understood me. I had a feeling you would, but for a moment, I worried you wouldn't."

Aubergine gave her a curious look and guided her through the fog. "Many things are perplexing, Cecelia. But my understanding of you is not one of them."

In the car, a clump of freshly pulled daisies lay across the dash. Cecelia chose a strand of her hair and gnawed. When the strand tried squirming away, she held tighter.

Unable to hold her questions any longer, she finally asked, "This is about Mother, isn't it? Tuesday's finally gotten to her, hasn't it?"

Aubergine stayed quiet so long, his silence grew around them like cobwebs, pinning them inside the car. After a deep breath, he answered, "She's gone, Cecelia."

"Gone?" Cecelia stuffed her hands into her sleeves and hugged herself tight. Her eyes stung with more stupid tears. She used to be brave—fighting invisible monsters with her Joan of Arc replica sword, daydreaming about sailing away on more adventures. But now nothing made sense, not even herself. "What do you mean, gone?"

"She left to look for your brother in the Land of Yesterday. She just couldn't stand being away from him any longer. I told her I was working on a way we could all go together. An invention I'd been working on for years but never had reason to perfect until . . . until Celadon left us. But a taxi had already come for her, and wouldn't wait." He met Cecelia's eyes. "I'm afraid that if your mother does find him, she might not return."

No! Cecelia thought fiercely. *No, no, no!*

Her mother had suffered terrible despair since her brother's death, during which time she barely spoke to Cecelia at all. But she never thought she'd leave; despite everything, Cecelia never thought her mother would leave *her.*

"Why didn't you go after her—why didn't you stop her?" Cecelia clenched her fists and willed back stinging tears. "How could you just let her go?"

Lightning flashed across the darkening sky.

"I did everything I could to convince her to stay. But sometimes, despite our best efforts, people leave anyway, even when we don't want them to." He poked the tip of her nose. "Besides, how could I leave without you?"

Thunder rolled overhead. It reminded Cecelia of her mother's laughter during summer downpours. How whenever thunderstorms moved over Hungrig, she and her mother would race outside onto the hill and dance in the rain until they were soaked and their cheeks hurt. Laugh until they fell to the grass and cried tears of joy. Now she might never hear her mother's laughter again.

Cecelia's heart twisted like a bloody rag.

She never even said goodbye.

THE TRAGEDY OF CELADON IGNATIUS DAHL

Monday prior to the first evil Tuesday had been typical. Cecelia had spent the early morning cutting out paper dolls and shouting at her brother to go away. After school, she'd played outside—dressing up the neighbor's cat, Fresno, in his favorite bonnet of flowers, stars, and swirls. Come twilight, her father called her indoors.

"Looks like our fun has come to an end, Sir Fresno the Wicked, but tomorrow is coattails-and-hat day, don't forget." Cecelia—reluctantly—dehatted Fresno, while her hair patted the tabby's sleek black fur. "See you tomorrow!" Cecelia shouted as she and Fresno skidded away in opposite directions.

"Father?"

"Up here, Cecelia," Aubergine called from her bedroom. What was he doing in there? As much as she loved her parents, she despised her parents entering her room. Every adventurer needed a sanctuary—a place to unwind from adventuring—and Cecelia's bedroom was hers.

As she stomped up the staircase, plaster dust rained from the walls. Widdendream huffed and puffed and struggled to patch the deepening cracks as Cecelia clomped her way up.

Aubergine Dahl stood in the center of her rug—or rather, in the center of a pile of clothes and yarn and paper and shoes and books and trash and cups and plates and art and sandwich crusts—shaking his head. "It's a wonder you find your bed among this rubbish," her father said while taking extrahigh steps out of the pile of refuse. "You'll need to clean this up before bed. Understand?"

Cecelia scowled; her traitorous hair gave a clap. For some reason, it enjoyed cleaning messes. "But—"

"Clean your room now, or no new books—library books included—for three months." The devilish man crossed his arms with a smirk. "Take it or leave it."

He knew perfectly well she'd always take that deal. In the end, she grunted, "Fine."

"Excellent." Without another word, her father left Cecelia (and her hair) to her work.

Once she (and her hair) had finished cleaning, Cecelia burst out of her bedroom on her way to brush her teeth when she spied the freshly polished banister. The wood gleamed in the hall lights like a wave beneath a full moon, begging to be surfed. Her hair pulled toward it, echoing Cecelia's craving, itching for a ride, too.

Needing no more convincing, Cecelia did the thing she'd been warned not to do more than any other not-to-do thing. She grabbed onto the knob at the top of the staircase banister, pulled herself up, and balanced the rail like a surfer. After a minute of imagining herself dominating the world's biggest wave, she readied to slide down the railing all the way to the bottom. Except, while lowering herself, her foot slipped and knocked the banister knob to the floor.

"Oh souls." The broken knob bounced loudly on the landing and stopped.

Her mother would not be impressed.

"Cecelia?" her mother called up from the kitchen. "What was that sound?"

In a flash, Cecelia leaped down, grabbed the broken knob, and set it gingerly back into place. "Nothing, just . . . cleaning my room."

"Hmm," her mother grumbled loudly. "You're not breaking anything up there, are you?" Cecelia had become an expert at breaking things: slicing sword marks into walls, lobbing various items through glass windows, carving famous historical quotes into bookshelves and hearths. And Widdendream had always cleaned up after her.

While searching for an excuse to give her mother (how did she always know everything anyway?), she overheard her brother downstairs. "It sounded like she broke the banister knob," Celadon told their mother. "She was probably rail-surfing again."

Cecelia gritted her teeth. Would he never stop bothering her?

As usual, Mother not only saw through her ruse, but also took her brother's side. "Cecelia, if you were rail-surfing again and broke the banister knob, then you'll need to glue it back on yourself—now, please."

The walls rattled and groaned.

Although Widdendream rarely spoke, Cecelia had gotten quite good at reading its grumblings, and right now, she knew just what it wanted. "But listen to Widdendream moaning. I think it wants to fix the knob itself."

For years, Widdendream had taken pride in keeping up with its own repairs, no matter how daunting: straightening its twisted gutters, rebuilding wonky steps, patching cracked walls, cleaning the basement after Aubergine's experiments exploded. However, unbeknownst to Cecelia, the older the house grew, the harder keeping up became.

If it weren't for Mazarine, who'd grown up inside Widdendream and remained its closest friend, its spirit may have left years ago.

Their home would do anything for her.

"Widdendream," Mazarine called throughout the house, "I know you'd rather repair yourself, but you've had a hard time doing that lately. So please, you'll let Cecelia fix the banister, won't you . . . for me?"

The house coughed and shook, yet eventually stilled and replied, "Anything for you . . ."

"Great, then it's settled." Mazarine hollered up to Cecelia, "Widdendream promises not to interfere."

Cecelia groaned. "Fine." Then she hugged the banister tight and whispered, "I'm sorry I broke you, old friend. But I'll let you fix yourself if you want? It can be our little secret." The hallway lights flared. Cecelia took that for a yes. "Wonderful, then—" Widdendream hacked another puff of dust. Cecelia furrowed her brow. "Hmm, you *do* seem a bit under the weather. How about I check on you before bed? If you can't fix it yourself, I will. *I promise.*"

Later that evening, Cecelia fell into a book, and later, into the land of dreams, never thinking of the broken banister knob again.

Until just after midnight on that first evil Tuesday, when

16

Cecelia's little brother, nine-year-old Celadon Ignatius Dahl, fell down the stairs from the second floor and broke. Though Cecelia didn't realize it at the time, she had heard the whole thing.

A muffled *thud-thud-thud* occurred beyond her closed bedroom door. The grandfather clock downstairs ticked and tocked. Cecelia flushed with sweat and sprang up in bed. She thought that maybe she heard a small startled cry. However, her blankets were warm and her floors cold, and she decided she'd had a bad dream. So, Cecelia closed her eyes, pulled up her covers, and quickly fell back to sleep.

Come dawn, her mother would find Celadon's body. She would wail until the walls cracked deeper and floors shook. Mazarine would shout at Cecelia for not fixing the banister, and for hearing Celadon fall and not trying to save him, which Cecelia admitted to in her shock and sorrow. Aubergine would cry and wrap Cecelia in his arms while waiting for the ambulance to arrive.

And Cecelia would force herself to look at Celadon, so quiet now, no more laughter, no smiles. She would whisper, "You looked up to me, and I failed you." Her hair would try to comfort her. But Cecelia, feeling undeserving of such love, would push it away. Then she would bid her brother one final goodbye. "Celadon, daisies will always remind me of you."

From that moment on, each time her heart beat, she would remember that Celadon had died because of her. And no matter how much she wanted to forget this horrible truth, she knew she never could.

Hours later, her mother locked herself in the bedroom and cried. Her father retreated to the basement. Alone, Cecelia stole to the attic. It was the room that held each house's spirit, and the perfect place to tell Widdendream how sorry she was for breaking her promise.

When she arrived, she found the door had drastically changed. The wood had turned funeral black. It crawled with scary-looking vines. Cobwebs and hissing spiders scurried about each rusted hinge. This didn't look like grief to Cecelia, but resentment and fear and rage.

She listened at the door, and overheard her house sobbing and muttering angrily, which she'd never heard it do before. "How could you? It's *your* fault. I curse you, curse you, *curse y*—"

Cecelia knocked. Spiders nipped at her knuckles; she listened and swiped them away. When no response came, Cecelia pushed open the door.

"Widdendream?" The inner room was dim. She took careful steps inside. Each ancient Dahl artifact had been overtaken with grime, stink, and thin black vines. Green poisonous-looking mist climbed the sunbeams like motes. The air was ice cold. All at once, Cecelia was sure: Widdendream had been muttering about her.

"I know you don't want to see me. That you must blame me like everyone else for what happened." Fat tears sprung to her eyes; her long hair brushed them away. "I just wanted to say I'm sorry. I promised to check on you, fix your banister if you couldn't, and I didn't keep my promise. Celadon's fall—it's all my fault."

Widdendream cried out in pain, "You promised. You fell asleep, and our boy died!" It shook, and then groaned in agreement, "Yes, you're right, so very right. It *is* all your fault."

"I swear," Cecelia sobbed, backing out of the attic in tears. "As long as I live, I'll never hurt you again."

Too ashamed to apologize to her mother, Cecelia entered Celadon's room. It still smelled like him—like the lake, summer breezes, and earth. She wrote her brother a letter with her wonderfully special pen in a fit of horror and tears, expressing how sorry she was. About how much she missed him. How desperately she wished she could hear him say "Sweet dreams, Cee-Cee" just one more time. How she longed for those rare days when they used to laugh instead of fight, when Celadon would giggle so hard he honked, which made them laugh even harder. She wrote about how scary it was to feel all alone. How she wanted someone to love her as her brother always had, even when she was disagreeable. She begged him repeatedly to come home, then signed her letter:

Thank you for loving me anyway.

I miss you,

Cee-Cee

Next, she placed the envelope under his pillow, hoping the letter she wrote would perform a miracle and find her brother in the Land of Yesterday. Yet when Cecelia woke, her note remained unclaimed, unopened, and unread.

She wrote more letters on more days, all with her special pen, and all of which suffered the same undeliverable fate. Cecelia swore she felt her heart shatter, and the wind whisper, *"For you, Cecelia Dahl, this day may never end."*

And it hadn't.

For Cecelia, Tuesday remained evil, and yesterday hung on like a vulture, refusing to let her go.

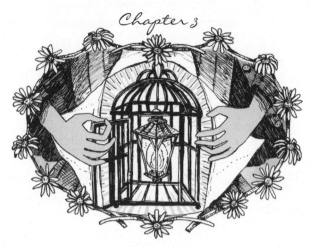

THE HOUSE OF WIDDENDREAM

Aubergine drove on in silence. As he approached their driveway, Cecelia noticed Widdendream looked more crooked and decayed than it had earlier that morning. Their home hunched like an old man in a wrinkled suit. Mold snaked the exterior of the attic. Widdendream's gutters stuck out willy-nilly like furious eyebrows. As decrepit as her home had become in recent years, Widdendream had never looked threatening until now.

Suddenly, candles lit in the attic windows with an ugly green light. Prickles of dread ran up and down Cecelia's spine.

How did they get lit?

She knew no one was home.

The car turned onto their driveway, and their neighbor, Mr. Curmudgeon, who was always shouting at someone about something, rushed at their car from the street. He pointed at them and shouted, "??? ???? ?? ???? ????? ?? ??????!" Cecelia froze. "What's gotten into him?" Aubergine asked with a blank expression. She wondered if her father could understand Mr. Curmudgeon's words, or if he only heard barking honks, too.

"Word farts," she wanted to reply, but answered, "I don't know," instead. Because what if he didn't believe in Wordfartopotamus Syndrome, or simply thought she was losing her mind? Then maybe he'd send her away, to one of those houses for those who'd lost their minds completely, and she'd never see him again.

She could not let that happen.

Mr. Curmudgeon's house spirit, which was as crotchety as its resident, flashed its lights in a fury. Each beam pointed accusingly at Widdendream. After one last frightened look, their neighbor hurried fast as a herd of turtles to his house, propelled himself inside, and slammed the door.

Cecelia's father parked the car. For a moment, neither exited the vehicle, only stared wide-eyed at the dark house. It looked so sinister. Cecelia guessed Widdendream must be taking her mother's leaving as hard as they were.

Side by side, they approached the front door. The attic windows, shaped like triangles with points as sharp as butcher's knives, seemed to glare down at them. Vile shadows danced past the glass in the candlelight. A beat later, the shadows had gone.

The door creaked open. Her father flipped the light switch, but the lights would not turn on. The sole illumination was a mazarine-colored mist, the same shade as her mother's eyes, snaking their feet. A foul stench plagued the foyer, like decomposing greenery. Their boots echoed across the floor.

"Mazarine . . . ," Widdendream groaned. "Celadon!" it cried next, and pounded the walls.

Thud, thud, THUD.

Thud, thud, THUD.

Fear dug in its fangs.

"Mazarine . . ." The walls moaned so quietly, Cecelia had to strain to hear. "I can't live without you. My light, come back to me!"

Narrowing his eyes at the walls, her father turned on the stairs. "Cecelia, did you hear that?" Aubergine glanced down into the foyer, head cocked, listening.

Cecelia removed her special pen from her pocket and drummed it anxiously on her thigh. Each mournful plea made her feel worse. "I did. It's Widdendream."

Her father shook his head. "It can't be. House spirits only talk to themselves when they've gone mad." Aubergine patted the banister. "Our Widdendream might be upset, but it wouldn't go mad, would you, Widdendream?" He sighed dramatically and continued up the stairs. "It must just be the ghost of your mother's absence I hear."

Widdendream laughed—a cruel and frightening laugh, so unlike its usual gentle spirit. The staircase swayed, yet Aubergine didn't seem alarmed. He glanced back at Cecelia with a weary look of either love or shame—she couldn't tell anymore.

The purple-blue mist whispered, "Murderer. Payback. *Revenge . . .*"

Hair hiding behind her back, Cecelia called after him, "Wait! Father, don't go!" Fresh mist bloomed from the walls.

"Cecelia." Her father peered at her over his shoulder. "I understand you're hurting. I am, too. But I was up all night and I'm so tired, I can't think straight." He rubbed his face with one hand. "If we're going to figure out where we go from here, I need to rest. Maybe you should do the same."

Frozen in place, Cecelia covered her ears and shut her eyes. She didn't know if she'd heard Widdendream whispering those horrible things or if she'd imagined it. Clearly it was upset that her mother left, and was still grieving Celadon's death, but she thought, under all its pain, Widdendream loved her anyway.

When Cecelia was little, she used to come home and fall into Widdendream's comfy library chair. It had become her refuge after her classmates had teased her about her curious freckles, strange interests, and, more often than not, her know-it-all cleverness, which often got the best of her. The chair would wrap her in its arms and Widdendream would read her stories of faraway lands and famous explorers: of Sea Captains, the Gnomes of the Stratosphere of Now, and the mythical Guardians of Yesterday. Whenever the crueler children made Cecelia feel like nothing, Widdendream had a way of making her feel like something again. Her home had helped her understand what it meant to be brave. Now it made her afraid.

"How could you rest at a time like this?" Cecelia cringed at the rotten stink inside the darkened house and stepped closer to the base of the stairs. "Why did you get me out of school early if you wanted to be alone?"

Aubergine gave her a weary smile. "It's Tuesday, a treacherous day for the Dahls at the best of times, but now . . . I just needed to know you were safe, that's all." He started back up the stairs. "And where could be safer than home?"

In the background, Widdendream growled, "Revenge!"

How could her father not hear it?

"But—"

"No buts, sweetheart. Go to your room and rest. We'll make a plan later, okay?"

Cecelia didn't know what to do. She didn't want to let her father out of her sight, but what choice did she have? Adults always did what they wanted, despite their children's sensible suggestions.

"Fine," she grudgingly complied.

And softly, Widdendream laughed.

The feeling of wrongness followed Cecelia upstairs, past the top step, from which her brother had fallen, and the banister knob, which her father had fixed. It dogged her heels by the small table on the second-floor landing that once held a fresh vase of daisies. It moved with her past the fractured walls, yet, to her relief, the threatening voices seemed to have ceased.

Inside Cecelia's bedroom, everything looked the same—same bed, desk, and chair, same shredding wallpaper, the same Cecelianess of her things. The garland of paper dolls strung from her ceiling still taunted her with memories of her brother. The familiar hauntedness of her room filled every inch of space.

She tried turning on her lights, but they wouldn't turn on either. Cecelia stood by the window and let the overcast sky light her intergalactic map. It covered an entire wall. Looking at it usually helped her relax.

In the center of the giant map was her own small world, which included the town of Hungrig. The Stratosphere of Now, a wonderfully gassy asteroid belt, surrounded her planet and housed the brave souls who flew the mysterious Intergalactic Taxies to Yesterday: the infamous Aeronautic Gnomes. Only rarely did they show themselves. But when they did, it was always to help those in the direst need.

In the upper-right quadrant of her map hung a planet called Earth. The cosmic outlaw Stella the Invincible, who lived there for a while, said it mirrored Hungrig almost exactly. She even wrote one of Cecelia's favorite books, *Heroes of Earth*, which included one of her favorites, a girl called Joan of Arc. Infinite other planets and stars of all sizes, shapes, and colors dotted everywhere else. Yet, as grand as her map was, it, like every other she knew of, failed to contain the perilous and forbidden Land of Yesterday: the floating black desert where souls went when their bodies died—the land where Celadon lived now, and where her mother was currently headed.

Some claimed the Land of Yesterday didn't exist. The few

cartographers who did believe refused to put it on a map. When Cecelia had asked her father why, he'd told her, "If people knew how to get to Yesterday, they'd leave Today, and the world would be nothing but ghosts."

But if it didn't exist, as some claimed, then where were her mother and brother now?

All of a sudden, Cecelia burst into tears. Oh, how she hated that! She wanted her old heart back. It never *ached*, not like this. Six weeks and one day ago, it beat strong as a warrior; it took punches and did what it needed to survive. It most certainly didn't make her a weeping mess, scared of her own house, scared of her own self.

This made Cecelia angry.

She balled her fists and stomped about her bedroom glaring at the posters on her walls. Cecelia's favorite explorers and adventuring heroes pinned over her bed—Eric the Blue from Hungrig, Joan of Arc from Earth, and Mortavia the Wild from the Gamut of Question—made her angry. She'd bet her collection of ancient coins none of them ever cried. Her antique swords in the glass case beside her dresser made her angry. The stuffed animals and metallic trinkets her brother gave her—mythical beasts and elsewhere planets he knew she'd love—made her angry. Her books— stories of characters stronger, braver, and wiser than she was now—made her angry. But the paper dolls circling her ceiling like holiday garland made her angriest of all.

Cecelia made them the day before Celadon died. She yelled at him when he tried to touch them—how she wished she could take that back! She hung them up after his death to remind her of all the times she'd pushed him away, and how she would do almost anything to have him help her now. She fell to her knees and punched the floor. Tears and hair flying, Cecelia cried, "I wish I was a tearless paper doll so I could stop crying and feeling so much. I want to be heroic like I used to be!"

Heated tears pouring down her cheeks, Cecelia pounded the floorboards again and again. She hated everything and felt, all at once, that everything hated her back.

And then, from the place she'd struck the floor, a stain of blackness pooled, and spread. Everything inside her room shook. Spiked vines slithered through the cracks in the walls, like those she'd seen in the attic. Cecelia's hair coiled her neck, trembling. She sensed Widdendream's eyes on her.

"What do you want from me, Widdendream?" Cecelia howled and jumped to her feet. "How can I make you stop hating me?"

Widdendream thundered in reply, "It's your fault Mazarine is gone!" Dust and chunks of mortar flew from the quaking walls. Cecelia covered her head with her hands. "You drove her away! Now I'm dark and falling apart—can't you see?" Bits of ceiling crumbled and fell. "My best friend— the one who lit me up and never let me down—is gone, and it's all because of you!" The room inhaled a slow, shuddering breath, then exhaled in a blast of words, "BRING HER BACK TO ME!"

Cecelia thought her father would come running after that last explosion of noise, but her door remained shut. If her father didn't come to her, she'd need to go to him.

Cecelia bolted for the door.

Her dresser slid in front, blocking her way.

"No need to disturb him, Cecelia," Widdendream growled, amused. "You don't want him mad at you, too. Besides, I think you've disturbed his life enough already, don't you?"

Her chin quivered. She pushed her fists into her burning eyes. "I'm sorry I ruined everyone's lives. I'm sorry I broke the banister and forgot to fix it. I'm sorry for making Celadon and Mother leave. I wish I could take it all back, but I can't. There's nothing I can do!"

A board ripped from the wall and flew a centimeter above her head. Surprised, her hair raised with the wrath of a thousand midnight-blue snakes.

"My good, kind Mazarine," Widdendream moaned, its voice getting farther and farther way. "Find a way to bring her home, Cecelia, or you will be a very sorry little Dahl." A new crack formed in Cecelia's wall. It opened ominously beneath her eyelike windows, lifting at the corners.

Lightning struck over the lake. In the flash of electric light, Cecelia realized Widdendream was grinning. The sort of grin a dog makes before it bites.

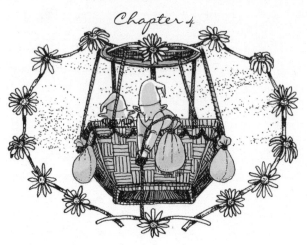

Chapter 4

THE MIRACULOUSLY MAGICAL PEN

The walls shuddered briefly, then stilled. The poisonous-looking vines and inky-black rot retreated through the cracks. Cecelia's pulse quickened and her hair flailed, crowding her neck. "Widdendream?"

She thought she heard a creak upstairs, but after that, nothing. Even the sour scent had left her room. She felt terrible, being responsible for someone else's darkness and pain as well as her own. Cecelia decided then and there: she would make a plan to get her mother back, for everyone's sake.

Right away, an idea took root. Cecelia removed her pen from her pocket, brushed remnants of plaster and dust from her desk, and sat. Then Cecelia remembered what her mother said as she gave her the remarkable pen: "This pen is a great gift, Cecelia. When combined with the ink of one's heart, it becomes powerful enough to bring writer and reader together, like magic."

When combined with ink of the heart. She'd forgotten about that part. *Maybe when I wrote Celadon's letters I didn't use the right kind of ink?*

"Okay, pen. I believed in you once. Now show me what I need to do to believe in you again." Cecelia placed the pen on her desk. For a few moments, it just sat there doing nothing but being a pen. But then, quick as you please, it stood up by itself, unscrewed its cap, unplugged the cork on its inner canister that held its ink, and turned upside down on its head.

Cecelia gasped. She'd never seen a pen do that before!

Wide-eyed, she watched as pale-blue ink ran over her desktop and drained onto the floor. The color reminded her of tears.

Tears.

The ink of one's heart.

Tears were the answer.

Cecelia picked up her empty pen and forced herself to imagine every pitiless memory haunting her: the thud in the dead of night, her brother at the base of the stairs, the looks of horror on her parents' faces when they found his body, her mother leaving, Widdendream's distress, her father's sorrow, the weakling she had become. Then she resurrected all the times she talked down to Celadon, screamed at him while he was still alive—"Go away!" "I hate you!" "I wish I never had a brother!" She remembered her mother laughing, rainy days, and daisies. How the light in her father's eyes went out when Celadon died, and how badly she wanted it back.

The pain was monstrous, like a beast devouring her heart. But she forced herself to feel it and channeled that pain into her tears. Cecelia cried, harder than she ever had before, until her tears poured like a great flood. And when her worst, never-want-to-remember memories reached their climax, she held the inner canister of her pen to the corners of her eyes, siphoned each drop into the tube, and then put her pen back together.

"This will work," Cecelia said as her hair dried her cheeks. "I know it will. I will write Mother a letter with these, my saddest and sorriest tears, and somehow, combined with the magic of my pen, this letter will find her in the Land of Yesterday. Maybe then she'll understand me and come home, and Widdendream will go back to being a friend."

Butterflies doing battle in her stomach, Cecelia opened her desk drawer. She removed a sheet of her best notepaper— shaped like a hot-air balloon and striped in a rainbow of color—and set her divine pen to page. She'd only written a handful of words when something within her changed.

The room became so quiet, Cecelia thought she heard the creak of a rusty door. Not from somewhere within the house, but from somewhere inside *her*.

The hairs on her neck stood on end.

She hunched over and listened harder. Cecelia swore she heard the clang-clang-clang of a brass knocker ring out behind her belly button—the sort of knock that belonged on a door.

"Hello?"

No answer.

Something inside her was different and she needed to know what it was. What if the magic she'd created by filling her pen with tears was inside her now and she needed to set it free?

Like opening a door.

Gooseflesh pinching her skin, Cecelia moved her chair back from her desk and gnawed the tips of her hair. Then, without thought of consequence, she picked up her pen of tears, and drew, in one continuous line over her gray-and-black-striped dress, a door, just above her belly button.

The tears from Cecelia's pen soaked through her dress and skin at once. Her middle tingled and cooled, then numbed.

The space within the door's borders thinned and stiffened and crinkled in a dreadfully paperish way.

Cecelia swallowed hard, her mouth dry as thousand-year-old bones.

"Is anything in there?"

With one middle finger, Cecelia tapped the curious door. When she did, her dress, and skin beneath it, dimpled and scrunched. Quickly, she drew back her hand, but it being evil Tuesday, Cecelia was too late.

The small door-sized piece of herself tore at the seams and opened, as if she was a three-dimensional paper doll. To Cecelia's astonishment, right beneath her dress door, hung another. This door, bordered by natural skin, was the same midnight blue as her hair, and as strong and translucent as a jewel. Remarkably, her middle didn't hurt a bit.

My pen is magic.

My pen is dangerous.

Cecelia tapped on the inner door of herself.

"Hello?"

The second door opened in reply.

Cecelia tried to see beyond her paper skin. A cool breeze billowed upward, scented with daisies, wind-dried linens, and the pages of old beloved books. Her unbuttoned sweater flapped like drapes. She anchored her hair and peered inside, as far into herself as possible. Behind the door, Cecelia found a miniature rusted lamp inside a tarnished Victorian birdcage. The bulb within her was as cold and dark as Widdendream, as if her light was broken, too.

A lock clicked. Cecelia gasped. The cage door opened with a slow and eerie *creeeak*. White wisps of frozen breath puffed when she spoke. "Hello?"

Cecelia waited for any reply.

A SURPRISE FROM THE OTHER SIDE

Many books about magical rabbit holes existed, and Cecelia had read them all. Yet none regarding paper girls or internal cages and doors inside paper girls came to mind. She couldn't be sure if her pen had created the lamppost and cage, or if they'd always been there. Did everyone who'd lost someone have a space like this inside, or was she the only one?

Peering into the icy darkness of herself, Cecelia noticed a tiny midnight-blue circle of skin alongside the door of her middle, not there a moment earlier. She ran a finger over the blue spot.

Paper.

Oh souls. Her paperness had spread. Just a little, but spread all the same.

Maybe using such a powerful tool as a miraculous tear-filled pen on herself wasn't such a great idea.

"Hello?" she asked again.

Cecelia received no reply. The only sound was the crinkling scrunch of her paper middle until the doors of herself slammed shut, and the ripped edges of her dress stitched together as if they'd never been torn.

Cecelia poked her middle, hoping she'd magically turned back to normal. But her dress, and the skin beneath it, remained as papered as ever. She listened at the door of herself a while longer, but heard nothing more.

Twisting a strand of her restless tresses, Cecelia considered calling out to her father. He could push the heavy dresser away from her door (if Widdendream let him). Also, as an inventor, maybe he'd know how to fix her paperness. But what would she say? She'd already caused so much trouble. What if he yelled at her for waking him, tired as he was? He might be the last person who loved her. She didn't want to drive him away, too.

She'd have to figure out her predicaments on her own.

"What would you do?" she asked the Joan of Arc action figure poised on her desk. "Any explorer worth her weight in adventure has to be built to last. If my paperness spreads and I crisp and dry, I'll never see Mother again, and Father will end up alone with angry Widdendream." Cecelia shook her head. "That is unacceptable."

She had to get her mother back.

Setting her jaw, Cecelia picked up her absolutely miraculous pen. Her only hope rested upon it and her tears, and the letter she'd write to her mother reaching the Land of Yesterday. Cecelia closed her eyes and tried to imagine the dreaded land. Legends claimed Yesterday wasn't a globe at all, but an enormous flat wasteland of black sands and skies, lost things and ghosts, hidden somewhere in deep space. Some said a haunted galaxy brimming with wormholes surrounded it. Others insisted the flip side of the black desert held the enchanted Sea of Tears—where every tear ever spent by every being ever born pooled in waters of lilac and gold beneath skies of crimson and tangerine. Lady and Lord Arnot of the Isle of Dragons maintained in their book, *Tales of Darkness and Light*, to have met the fierce Sea Captain who guarded the waters himself. If this legend of the Sea of Tears proved true, Cecelia's letter might reach Yesterday after all.

Finally, in a frenzy of feelings and words, Cecelia scratched her tears to page. She begged her mother's forgiveness and that she'd come home. Cecelia asked her mother why she left and why she didn't love her anymore and why she was so easy to leave. Cecelia wrote *I'm sorry* a million times. So consumed was Cecelia in the letter to her mother, she blocked out every sight and sound, every thought and worry, leaving just her and the outpouring of words. And in one final burst of energy, Cecelia signed her name and folded the letter into its envelope, done.

"Okay, Mother, you knew this pen was miraculous, and I believe my tears are the same." Cecelia stood, still focused on the envelope, and allowed a small grin of hope. "I wrote this letter for you. Now, if you love me, catch it!" On instinct, she tossed her letter high. It hit the ceiling and went straight through, blipping out of sight.

Magic.

Just as Cecelia opened her mouth to cheer, her letter reappeared. It plunged back through the ceiling and zigzagged in slow arcs to the floor. A small moan ran away with her smile. Her hair nuzzled her neck and wrapped her in a hug. "I don't understand."

Cecelia had felt certain that if she threw the special letter, her mother would catch it. It seemed logical that if a girl could turn into paper, and a pen could perform miracles, a letter of tears could reach the Land of Yesterday. *Maybe*, she thought determinedly, *I'll have to deliver the letter to Mother myself.*

While Cecelia retrieved her unanswered letter, a bolt of lightning struck outside. Her bedroom flashed white, illuminating her surroundings. She cast long, brow-furrowed gazes around her room. Cecelia's eyes popped wide as she realized what was wrong.

Oh souls.

Her sorrow had spread.

Cecelia's bedroom walls and shelves had become parchment thin. Her music box collection and every knickknack she owned had crisped and flattened into fancy rectangles of colorful origami. The desk she wrote on turned into hard black poster board. Her circular rug went from braided wool to elaborately woven cardboard. Her curtains, once gauzy and light, now hung at her windows in sheets of creased gray newsprint. She pressed a hand to her bed; it crackled like ice that froze too fast and made itself into paper. Each dress and shoe, figurine and stuffed toy, everything had turned to paper. But that wasn't the only thing that had changed.

She turned her letter over in her hands. Curiously, the envelope had transformed as well. It was now transparent, like tears.

Observing this odd new letter, she felt a sunny warmth fill her cage. A faint glow of pale-yellow light seeped through her paper skin and dress, and out into her bedroom.

My lantern, she thought. *It is lit.*

A sudden gust of arctic winds scourged toward her. Her newspaper curtains rustled sideways. Cecelia froze.

Mist in the shape of a person caught her eye across the room.

"No."

Cecelia held her breath, watching the impossible shape emerge through the wall.

"It can't be."

Her spine tingled and knees became weak.

"Are you . . . *real?*"

The last time she'd seen him, he had been lying in a coffin lined with immaculate white silk. He hadn't looked like himself; he had been wearing a suit; his hair had been neatly combed and his eyes closed; his smile had been stolen permanently. Cecelia's tears had landed on his artificially rouged cheeks. When she wiped them away, his chilled skin stabbed an icicle into her heart and she had been cold ever since.

"I'm as real as you are, Cee-Cee," the dark-haired boy with the hint of a smile replied. He stopped an arm's length away.

The air temperature dropped several degrees.

Delicately, afraid she would break the spell, Cecelia

touched his cheek. The lantern within her sparked and glowed in a spray of yellow and gold. The sudden warmth surging through her felt like coming back to life.

"Celadon," Cecelia whispered. "You're home."

A GHOST WITH PALE-GREEN EYES

Shaking with disbelief and nervous excitement, Cecelia blinked in stunned silence at her ghost brother. The boy who died because of her, whose death left a permanent hole in her family, had come home.

Celadon hovered above the floor in front of her. He looked almost as she remembered him: black hair, bronzed skin as dark as her own, and the loveliest pale-green eyes. Though he did seem older. The whole of him, including the suit and basketball shoes their parents had buried him in, glowed in a misty shade the same as his irises.

She'd imagined this moment at least a zillion times and had written him as many letters, pouring out her sorry heart for her role on that nefarious day. And now here they stood: one girl with papering skin, and one ghost of a boy. Suddenly, Cecelia didn't know what to say.

When she placed her hands on her brother's cheeks, they didn't go all the way through; his body held the texture of cotton candy and the bite of Hungrig snow. Her hair reached out to his, and lovingly ruffled the cool dark waves. Celadon laughed. Cecelia asked again, her mind not ready to believe, "Celadon, is it really you?"

"It's really me." A cockeyed smile she never thought she'd see again rose on his vaporous face. "I'm kind of a ghost. But I'm still kind of *me*, too."

"Oh, how I've missed you!" She pulled him into a fierce hug. A barb of guilt washed over her at feeling the realness and impossibleness of him. Yet no tears came. "I didn't want you to leave me."

Pulling away, Celadon patted the space over his heart. "I'm never all-the-way gone, Cee-Cee. No matter where I am, I'm never far from you."

Chin wobbling, Cecelia grinned and couldn't stop. "How did you get here? Have you come from the Land of Yesterday? Have you seen Mother? Is she with you?" Cecelia stepped back and grabbed his hands. She never wanted to let go.

"None of that matters right now," Celadon answered with

the seriousness of an adult. "I don't have much time here."

Cecelia's hair drooped. "What do you mean? You can't leave already—you just got home."

Celadon started to say something, when a door banged shut upstairs.

Maybe Father was awake? Cecelia wondered if he'd be able to see Celadon's ghost, too. If he could, that might convince him to accompany her to Yesterday. Then she and her father could bring Mother home together.

Celadon whispered into his sister's ear, "I've come to warn you. You're heading for a world of trouble."

Her hair curled around her shoulders like a sleek blue fox. Cecelia whispered back, "Is this about Widdendream?"

"Widdendream?" Celadon grew even paler and seemed lost in deep thought.

"Or is this about Mother and the letter I wrote her? Did she read it? Does this mean she's coming home?"

"Cee-Cee, please, just listen, okay? This is important, and I would've come sooner to tell you, but the land of the living is forbidden to the ghosts of Yesterday!"

Cecelia had never heard her little brother shout before. "Okay, I'm listening."

Celadon's eyes grew so intense she thought she'd drown in their icy-green glimmer. "After I caught—"

"After you caught my letter?" Cecelia clasped her hands at her chest. "*You* found it. That's why it returned so strange-looking. You caught it and then came to guide me to the Land of Yesterday so I could give the letter to Mother myself!" Cecelia and her hair hugged Celadon so tightly, his body squished like a marshmallow and his eyes bugged out of his head. Her paperish middle scrunched.

"No, that's not it!" Celadon drew away and lowered his voice. "It wasn't me who caught your letter. Truth is, I've come to stop you."

Thunder moved across the horizon like a bowling ball down an endless lane.

Cecelia narrowed her eyes. "*What* did you say?"

"I've come to stop you from going to the Land of Yesterday. And when I leave here, you mustn't follow."

"B-but," Cecelia stammered, "I don't understand— why?"

He motioned to her middle; lantern light glowed softly through her paper doors. "For one thing, just getting to Yesterday is half the battle, and too dangerous, especially in your delicate condition. You'll get yourself killed, or worse!"

"Delicate . . . condition?" Cecelia may not have been as brave as she once was, but she still didn't like being told what she could or could not do. "Listen to *me*, Celadon. I have to go to Yesterday. And since you know the way, *you* are going to take me."

He crossed his arms. "Out of the question."

"What about Mother? Aren't you worried about her? Don't you want her to come home?"

Celadon skated over the floorboards in lazy figure eights through a haze of mist. "My worry about Mother isn't the point. Right now, I'm worried about you." He sighed. "I've already broken the Law of the Dead by escaping to warn you. If I brought you back with me, who knows what the Guardian of Yesterday would do." Cecelia's hair flailed, crowding her neck. She'd forgotten about the Guardian of Yesterday: a ferocious feline as big as a giant. "There is another reason I came—something else I needed to tell you." Celadon paused his frantic pacing and tapped his chin. "Oh no, I'm forgetting again! The harder I try to remember what it is, the harder it is to remember. . . ."

Cecelia's lantern light flickered. "Does it have to do with the cage and lantern inside me? Or is it something to do with Widdendream being so angry?"

A mist of motes fell from Celadon's hair when he shook his head. "I'm not sure, exactly, but that's the second time you've mentioned Widdendream. Come to think of it, this house doesn't feel the nice way I remember it. It's almost as if Widdendream's haunted because—" He floated upward and thoughtfully touched the ceiling. A dreamlike expression crossed his face as he dragged his fingers along a deep, jagged crack. "Oh, that's it! I remember what I needed to tell you. It was—"

The walls shuddered and shook. Black mold flooded the floors. Whip-sharp vines clustered around them, ready to snap. Cecelia's belongings flew from shelves toward Celadon, and blew right through him. Her strand of paper dolls ripped from the ceiling and fell at her feet. When Cecelia glanced down at them, the floor tore up in a wave and sent her cartwheeling through the air. Celadon rushed to catch her, but her hair beat him to it. Midnight-blue strands stretched to the ground like an extra set of arms. They flipped her right side up and then plopped her back on her feet. All the paper things not bolted down had piled before the dresser at Cecelia's door: bed, bookshelves and books, sword case, swords, nightstands, and all Cecelia's clothes and shoes. It was like Widdendream was trying to keep Celadon from telling her something.

But what?

"ENOUGH!" Widdendream bellowed, and pushed the siblings apart. Everything inside the room stilled. "Cecelia's idea was sound," the house growled. "She *should* go to the

Land of Yesterday to pay for all she's done, and to convince Mazarine to come home. So you, you meddlesome pest of a boy, need to leave. Return to Yesterday immediately!"

Photographs of the Dahl family soared from shelves. They circled Cecelia, taunting her with the loveliness of days gone by. Cecelia snatched her mother's letter and pen of tears off her desk, stuffed them into her pocket, and turned to her brother.

"I'm sorry, Celadon. All of this is my fault. I never meant to hurt anyone. Not you, Mother and Father, or Widden-dream." Cecelia grabbed her brother's shoulders and stared into his misty green eyes. "I haven't even told you how sorry I am for what happened. How I never meant to—how I never wanted you to—"

Celadon's eyes jolted wide, his mouth opened in a silent scream.

"Celadon?"

Abruptly and unnaturally, her ghost brother's body was thrust backward, as if dragged by a force beyond his control.

Cecelia sped after him. "What's wrong?"

Celadon kicked and clawed for purchase, straining against the invisible hands heaving him toward the back wall. "Yes-terday. It's pulling me back."

"You can't go," Cecelia shouted. "You just got here!"

Every time she reached for him, he got farther away.

"I told you," he groaned, trying to slither free, "Yesterday doesn't like letting us go. Promise you won't follow me." Arms grappling air, legs desperate to grip the floor, Celadon met her eyes. "The Land of Yesterday is filled with dark magic, lost souls, and danger—for the living, and for the dead who disobey and escape."

"I'm sorry," Cecelia said as she pushed against the invisible force trying to stop her from reaching her brother. "But I can't promise that. I won't break any more promises." She didn't want to argue with him; he'd died because of her, after all. But if the Land of Yesterday was so treacherous, then she needed to get her mother out of there, now. "I'm going to the Land of Yesterday to find Mother, and nobody, not even you, can stop me."

Celadon reached the wall and braced against it. "You always were stubborn," he said with a ghost of a smile that vanished as fast as it came. "But Mother won't be the same as you remember her; Yesterday changes the living, and not for the better."

The ceiling flexed angrily. A blockade of paper debris fell between them. The weight of Cecelia's mistakes condensed around her like stone, and it seemed she'd never be free.

"Cee-Cee." Celadon reached his hands out to her as his

misted torso sank deeper into the wall. "Promise you won't go to Yesterday. Please, promise me!"

The fact that she was losing her brother before her eyes hit her like a sack of bricks. She couldn't let this happen, not again.

Cecelia dived under the pile of ousted drawers, paper clothes, stuffed animals, and swords, and scrambled toward her brother. Whatever had ahold of him didn't stop her this time. Cecelia clasped onto his misty hands. "I won't let you go again." Cecelia pulled him toward her as hard as she could. Her hair twined his wrists like vines. Cecelia laughed. "It's working!"

With a tentative smile, Celadon pushed off the wall with his elbows. Inch by inch, he moved deeper into the bedroom. "Yeah, you're doing it, maybe—"

A sharp BANG echoed from upstairs, trailed by a sharper cry.

Father.

Distracted, Cecelia lost her grip. Celadon's fingers slipped through hers. Her hair couldn't hold on.

No.

Cecelia stared at Celadon in horror. His body thinned to boy-shaped smoke and seeped farther into the wall. His hands still extended to her, he cried, "Cee-Ceeeee!"

She lunged to latch on. But when she reached for him, her hand hit the bare wall. And once again, just like that, her brother was gone.

Widdendream's cruel laughter surrounded Cecelia like an echo, vanishing as quick as it came. The lantern within her, lit since Celadon arrived, dimmed to a flicker, barely visible through her paper center.

"I couldn't save him." Cecelia rested her forehead on the area where her brother disappeared and banged her fists against it. "Why can I never save him?"

Her hair fell limp. Her face went slack. Loneliness filled every molecule of space. Cecelia stared at her paper things piled up at her paper door and then down at her own paper-ness. Now even more of her middle felt numb. Carefully, Cecelia opened the parchment door of her dress, and the result was as she feared. Another small section of her skin had papered alongside her inner door. Cecelia shivered and shut herself tight. Once more, the papered fabric of her dress sealed straightaway.

She wrapped her sweater around herself and hugged herself close.

No matter what Cecelia did, no matter how right she thought her actions, somehow, she always made things worse.

Chapter 7

INTO THE MONSTER'S MOUTH

"Regret is a scared bird chained inside Yesterday," her mother told her once. "Break the chains. Set it free. And I promise you, it will evolve into a bird of hope."

Whether Cecelia did as her ghost brother begged her or followed her heart to Yesterday, one thing had become clear: she needed to get away from Widdendream.

Be the bird, Cecelia, she told herself. *If you're going to get out of here, you'll have to break your own chains.*

"I thought he'd never leave," Widdendream thundered. "Now it's your turn to go."

"Cecelia!" her father cried out in alarm from somewhere upstairs.

"Father!" The lantern inside her cage flickered with heat and blazed back to life. A soft glow shone through her paper skin and dress. Cecelia aimed her voice toward the ceiling. "Father, are you all right?"

Shadows danced across her walls like marionettes, each one resembling her father being choked by shadowy hands. Upstairs, muffled words and angry shouts, followed by a crack, and a *thud, thud, THUD* prickled Cecelia cold.

"Hold on," Cecelia hollered. "I'm coming to you!"

Shredded bits of paper shorn from Widdendream's ceiling and walls fell fast and sharp and deepened in her room like snow. Paper drifts eclipsed the height of her cage and cut her as she plowed her way to the door.

Almost there, Cecelia thought she was home free, when a *rip* and a *pop* echoed behind her. The floor in the center of her bedroom puckered from the weight of the shredded paper. Everything inside her room slid toward the hole, including her.

"Cecelia?" her father shouted, sounding farther away and out of breath. He had to be in the attic. "What was that noi—" A wet *thump* cut him off.

Cecelia struggled to hang on, grasping at bits of flooring, along with her hair. "Widdendream, stop this!" The section she grabbed tore away, but she quickly found another.

"Mazarine was my heart," Widdendream wailed. "A body can't live without a heart! I'll die without her, Cecelia, and eventually fall into the ground." The back wall crunched into a face and sneered. "So, until you bring Mazarine back to me, Aubergine stays inside my walls." Widdendream laughed. "He makes an awfully good insurance policy, don't you think?"

A fireball of terror blew up in Cecelia's chest. Widdendream was trying to keep her from her father. Just like it was trying to keep Celadon from telling her certain things. But how could she save her family on her own?

All at once, the room angled down like a funnel. A hot, vile wind blew up through the hole in the center of the bedroom. In a slippery whoosh, the paper snow and furniture hurried toward Cecelia.

Determined to reach her father, she scaled her possessions like a leopard up a mountainside, refusing to look back. When she reached her door, she found it clear of debris. Cecelia grinned. Then, balancing on her trusty bookshelf, which had remained steadfast to the end, she broke open her door.

But her victory didn't last long.

The hallway hung with ripped sheets of paper. The red-and-black Victorian wallpaper drooped, and the ceiling pitched wildly toward the floor. Thorny plants crawled toward her. One tripped her and Cecelia stumbled. Spiders hissed and scuttled away. She grabbed a loose paper sword and tried slashing the vine in two. She hit it again and again but it wouldn't sever.

Cecelia ditched the sword. She leaped over the vines instead, ducking and swerving and hurdling until, eventually, she slipped free.

"You can't have him, wicked girl!" Widdendream bellowed. Cecelia coughed out paper and dust as she sped to the stairs. "And, to make sure you follow through on this promise, unlike the promises you made me before, wherever you go, I will follow." The hallway deflated and inflated like lungs. "I will be watching you."

She needed to figure out a way to distract Widdendream long enough to reach the attic and her father inside it.

Eureka.

Talking made an excellent distraction.

"Widdendream," Cecelia said, tiptoeing up the staircase toward the third floor, "do you remember when Celadon and I used to sneak out after dark to stare at the stars? You used to sing to our parents to keep them asleep." Widdendream used to say the best magic happened when adults slept and kids were awake. Cecelia missed its gentle soul.

Widdendream made retching noises from every point in

the house. "That was before you and the boy outgrew me, and stopped spending time with me—before that first despicable Tuesday. Before you made me a monster!"

Ignoring Widdendream's nastiness, Cecelia crept up the attic stairs. "That's not true, Widdendream. Celadon and I loved you. No matter what, we always came home to you." She'd made it to the attic door. Ugly black vines coiled over the doorknob. She shoved them away and tried turning it; the door was locked from the inside. Cecelia frowned. "But now you're acting like an evil house with a scar where your heart used to be."

Widdendream inhaled deeply and let its breath out in a growl. "You have never been more right."

The parchment lightbulb in the cramped stairwell surged with electricity and exploded. Sparks sprayed. Bits of paper smoldered to the floor. The vines scurried down the stairs for shelter.

Widdendream said no more.

"Cecelia?" her father called quietly through the door.

"Yes," she answered. "Are you okay?" Cecelia tried the knob again—still locked. Her hair slithered under the crack for a peek, and returned more anxious than ever.

"The house has turned ugly," Aubergine said quickly. "It's locked me in. I can't seem to find a way out. When I try, it—" Her father abruptly stopped speaking.

Cecelia glared at the house. "Is Widdendream . . . hurting you?"

"Something like that. What about you? Are you all right?"

The question gave her hives. How could she tell him she'd found a cage with a lantern inside her? Or that she was covered in thorn pricks and cuts? Or that part of her was slowly turning to paper? She hated to do it, but she had to lie to protect him.

"I'm perfectly fine," Cecelia replied. "I'm going to try to open the door."

"Be careful. Widdendream's lost its mind—" Her father stopped himself short.

Violent shadows danced under the doorjamb. She thought she heard Widdendream whisper "Shut up," and "Be still," and "You lied. . . ."

Cecelia's hair trembled with fear. She patted it until it stilled. "What's going on in there?" She kicked the door again and again. And then Cecelia smelled smoke.

"Cecelia!" Aubergine shouted breathlessly. "I'm . . . Everything's fine. Listen to me. You're going to have to be especially brave now. Can you do that for me?"

As she opened her mouth to answer, a curl of smoke rose between her feet. Cecelia glanced down. The sparks from the broken light had eaten a hole through the floor. Her stomach dropped. And a breath later, so did she.

Grabbing onto a dangling section of flooring, Cecelia hung on. Part of her hair stretched up and dug into the floor-boards like anchors, while another part extinguished the smoldering flames. Cecelia didn't dare scream, not wanting to frighten her father.

"Talk to me, Cecelia!" Aubergine banged on the wall beyond the door. "Let her go, you monster, or I swear—" His voice cut off midthreat.

"Father, yes. I'm okay!" Cecelia answered. He had other things to worry about besides her dropping into a black void. *"You're going to have to be especially brave,"* he had said. She spun his words into a mantra, setting them on a loop in her mind. Cecelia hadn't been truly brave in so long, she wasn't sure if she remembered how. But this was her *father*. She had to do something.

Slowly and steadily, with the help of her faithful and daring blue hair, Cecelia pulled herself up and over the hole. She climbed onto a thin strip of flooring in front of the attic's entrance, found her balance, and heaved a huge sigh of relief.

Behind her, a sheer drop opened into a black abyss, no sign of anything below. In front of her stood a door she couldn't open with perhaps the last living person who loved her trapped on the other side.

"Cecelia, listen closely." Her father choked out the words as if in pain. "There's a hot-air balloon outside heading toward us. You'll recognize the drivers as Aeronauts, as discussed in our *Unbelievable Encyclopedia of Otherwhere Travelers* book." *Aeronauts. From the taxi service to Yesterday—here?* "Your mother caught one like it earlier. Now that you're here, I can . . . yes, I can try to make a break for the window. Then we can go after her together. Find a way onto that balloon, and I'll do the same." After a silence, he said, "Sweetheart, you're going to have to trust me."

Cecelia trusted him unconditionally. "Yes, escape into the balloon. Got it."

But not before I try to get you out one last time.

"Good girl."

The house cackled, evil as a sharp-toothed witch. Downstairs, furniture crashed and smashed against walls. Foul breezes blew up the stairwell. Cecelia's hair curled against her neck a bit too tightly.

"Cecelia," Aubergine shouted. "Get out of here, now!"

She gave the door one last shove, trying desperately to open it. Hard paper boards from inside the walls broke loose and grabbed Cecelia like arms, pinning her against the attic door. A vine wrapped her ankle; she crushed it under her boot and it skittered away. "Sorry, Cecelia," Widdendream moaned on a hot snap of wind. "Aubergine stays with me."

The armlike boards that had pinned Cecelia bit into her sides.

Cecelia wondered: if Widdendream had her father, what if he couldn't get away?

"Widdendream," Aubergine pleaded. "Please, it doesn't have to be this way—"

A crack, smash, and a groan issued from the attic, followed by a dreadful silence.

"Father?"

No reply. Maybe her father had already escaped out the window.

Or maybe Widdendream had knocked him out cold.

A determined fire pulsed and blazed in her belly as she fought against her constraints. Widdendream snarled and held her tighter. In an explosion of speed, Cecelia's blue hair ripped the armlike boards from the wall and snapped them in half. The house roared like dragons in battle. Debris sprayed up through the hole in the floor.

Free from Widdendream's grip, Cecelia lunged at the attic door, but it still wouldn't open. She needed to get to the balloon.

Cecelia spun around. She scanned the chasm before her.

She would have to jump the break.

Coughing on paper dust, Cecelia pictured her mother's face. She could almost smell her perfume. Hear the voice she knew before she took her first breath. Cecelia thought of her father and the beat of his heart when she laid her head on his chest. This gave her the strength to jump.

When she was halfway across the gorge, the house shifted. The rest of the landing gave way. Cecelia plummeted into the darkness.

Quick as whips, her hair twined any available surface, giving Cecelia time to latch on. Below her, sour winds raged faster. Every muscle in Cecelia's arms trembled with strain. Outside the house, something mechanical whirred in a loose gust of wind.

Glancing down through the hole in the floor, Cecelia thought about what her father had said: about the hot-air balloon outside and that she had to trust him. If jumping downstairs was her only escape, then she was going to have to jump. She would figure out how to find Father and the balloon afterward.

"Let go," she told her hair.

Her hair trusted her and let go.

Cecelia dangled by five fingers, four fingers, three—then none, and plunged into the monster's mouth.

Chapter 8

THROUGH THE RABBIT HOLE

Cecelia tumbled and banged as she fell, breaking through two parchment floors before hurtling into the basement. She passed shelves of glowing clocks, telescopes, sextants, buzzing gadgets, and mysterious maps (some made entirely of secret tunnels), when one of her books, *Tales of Darkness and Light*, opened a foot from her face. The left page showed a fearsome beast called the Caterwaul, Cat Guardian of the Land of Yesterday. The right displayed a weathered man in a yellow coat and hat known as Captain Shim, Guardian of the Sea of Tears—a body of water abloom with daisies on the flip side of Yesterday one couldn't cross without falling off the edge of the world. He rowed a small white boat and stared boldly back at her. Cecelia swore she saw him wink.

The next second, the book snapped shut and dived into the dim below, toward the quickly approaching floor.

Hair whipping wildly, Cecelia searched for something to grab on to. The lever of an odd-looking machine, riddled with buttons, knobs, and lights, jutted from the wall to her right. No matter how many times she'd asked, her father wouldn't tell her what the machine was for, yet had insisted she not touch it. Except now she had no choice.

Cecelia grasped hold of the lever. She swung there for a moment, and even plotted climbing the shelves to the top, when the handle lowered, the machine clicked, and her hand slipped.

"Oh souls," Cecelia muttered as the basement floor fell away beneath her.

In its place was a tunnel, a yard in diameter, that resembled a silver-gray covered slide. Cecelia slid down the chute twisting this way and that. Tiny, luminous, wiggly things poked from the misted channel walls. When she looked closer, she saw they were worms. This was a wormhole. Years ago, her father had attempted to create such a thing. He'd worked on it for years, but gave up, saying, "It's more difficult than you might think. I can only get it to go to one place, and it's nowhere I want to be." That must be the machine he'd been working on in the basement since Celadon died.

Exactly one scream later, Cecelia poured through the end of the tunnel and out the other side.

Cecelia cartwheeled through a shimmering orange-red sky toward a purplish-goldish daisy-filled sea. A man wearing a yellow raincoat and hat, sitting in a small white rowboat, watched her fall. With a volcanic splash, Cecelia plunked into the boat, right side up on the seat. The vessel rocked; water sprayed her skin. The raincoat man smiled serenely from the bench in front of her. He had long white whiskers laced with purple lightning bolts. His eyebrows were so bushy Cecelia could have knit them into mittens. To match his rain gear, he wore galoshes to his knees. She recognized him immediately as Captain Shim, Guardian of the Sea of Tears on the flip side of Yesterday.

Like from her book.

Cecelia should have been horrified, startled at the very least, at plummeting through Widdendream into this nether-world via a wormhole in her basement. But here, now, in this calm, otherwise place, for some reason, she merely felt curious about the Sea Captain. Maybe he knew the way back to her father and the balloon waiting for her.

"Hello there, Cecelia." Miniature bolts of lightning

zapped through his beard. He took the oars and began to row.

Since he didn't speak in trumpets and honks, Cecelia concluded, the Sea Captain had lost loved ones, too.

"Hello, Sea Captain." She gazed across the daisy-coated sea; the small white flowers reminded her of her mother. Cecelia cleared the emotion from her throat and looked the Sea Captain in the eye. "May I ask how you know my name?"

"Oh, that's easy," he replied in a voice gruff as a storm. "I know everyone's names. You're the Daughter of Paper and Tears, and you're headed for the Land of Yesterday."

That sounded about right. "You certainly know a lot of mysterious things."

"I do. But what I'm permitted to tell visitors is quite limited."

"How about this?" Cecelia asked, hair spooling around her in relaxed blue waves. "If you know me so well, are you also familiar with my father, Aubergine Illustrium Dahl? We were about to begin our journey together, when I dropped here through a wormhole in our basement. I don't want to leave him behind."

"Good old Aubergine." The Captain smiled and continued to row. "I'm aware of your family's situation, sure, and of your father's passageway. He's traveled through it many times seeking someplace else." He paused. "I am sorry you have to go through this confusing and crazy ordeal, Cecelia. Unfortunately, confusing and crazy ordeals are often the only way to get to the bottom of incomprehensible things."

Cecelia weighed the Guardian's words. Though she didn't want them to be true, she felt they were all the same. She couldn't explain how exactly, other than to say things *here* and *now* seemed especially *true*.

"However," Captain Shim continued, "if you keep your eyes and ears open, I could help you find a way back to your family."

"Really?"

"Sure." When the Captain took his hands off the oars, the oars rowed on without him. This Captain was quite magical. "The only way to leave the Sea of Tears is to truly want to be in Today. Focus on where you wish to go, picture it clearly in your mind, and when you're ready to leave, trust the sea to show you the way."

Cecelia smiled. The daisies bobbed happily upon the water. Everything here felt good. The Captain, the sea—it was all so peaceful. The more she calmed, the warmer her middle became. "One more question: Do you know anything about papering girls with cages and lanterns inside them, Captain Shim?"

The oars stopped rowing. The Captain burst into laughter. "Well, sure I do! Every Guardian knows that." He leaned closer as if to share a top-secret secret. "All I can tell you is this: only those who've been sad enough to write letters with their unhappiest tears can turn into paper and see such miracles. The trick is remembering what makes you shine. Although I have no doubt you'll find your answer in time."

Cecelia furrowed her brow. "Do you know how long that will take, Sea Captain?"

"You'll have to find that out for yourself." Shim's irises changed from blue to gold. The closer she looked at him, the more she saw. How his skin seemed to glow, ever so slightly, like the sun. How the daisies drew to him with absolute trust, how he radiated an infectious joy. "All I can say is that a lot of people are counting on you to make it through the Land of Yesterday and out the other side."

"Like Mother and Father, and Celadon?"

Shim smiled dubiously.

"Can you at least tell me if Father made it into the Aeronaut's balloon?"

"I'm afraid that's for you to find out."

Daises flocked to Cecelia's side of the boat. They formed the shape of a hand and waved her forward. Next, they rearranged into the figure of a child with long, excitable hair and dived into the depths of the sea.

Cecelia looked to Captain Shim. His tangled eyebrows rose daringly.

Like a challenge.

Cecelia peered over the side of the rowboat. A single daisy rose from the place the others vanished. Cecelia reached out and stroked its petals. The instant she touched it, a flash of memory struck her—of the vase of daisies at the top of Widdendream's second-floor landing. How her mother had filled it the day before Celadon died. How, when he fell, it fell with him, and daisies and water and death followed him down.

Cecelia dropped the flower and folded her hands. She glanced at the other daisies spilling out across the horizon and pictured her father in the car this morning. How in his grief over her mother's leaving, he'd yanked up a clump of Dahl daisies and set them on the car's dash to remind him of her.

Daisies. Daisies. Daisies.

They almost felt like a clue.

Maybe if she followed their trail, like bread crumbs through the dark woods, they would lead her back to where she belonged. But how could she dive into the water with paper skin? Wouldn't the Sea of Tears rip her apart?

To save her parents, it was worth a try.

"Thank you for speaking with me, Captain Shim." Cecelia smiled and buttoned her sweater. "I think I've figured out what to do."

"Anytime," Captain Shim replied, grasping the oars.

Cecelia closed her eyes and envisioned Hungrig. She remembered the mountains and sky, and her father and the hot-air balloon waiting for her at home, right now.

And Cecelia dived into the sea, hair first.

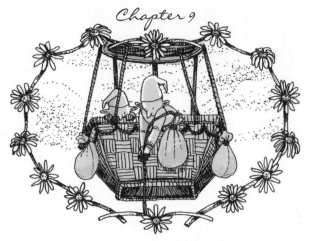

THE DRÖM BALLONG AND TWO
VERY CURIOUS GNOMES

Cecelia screamed. As soon as she dived into the sea from Captain Shim's boat, the water transformed into starlit space. She tumbled and sank past stars in a wet tangle of daisies and hair, no wormhole tunnel in sight.

Cecelia stopped screaming to catch her breath.

The mechanical whirring she'd heard earlier while inside Widdendream rose all around her as she fell through clouds and sky. The popping *PSSH* sound of forced air followed. The clouds cleared to reveal a miraculous sight below: a rainbow-striped hot-air balloon soaring up from the ground to meet her.

Father! This had to be the balloon he said they'd escape in together. It looked just as she'd pictured it before plunging into Captain Shim's sea. Surging with hope and joy, Cecelia dived toward the hot-air balloon, midnight-blue hair trailing her like a cape. Her father had to be in the basket waiting for her.

The closer she got, the more she saw. Two petite men wearing bright vests and purplish-blue hats peered up at her from the basket's edge. Cecelia drew in a fast breath.

Oh souls. *It really is them!*

Just that morning in class, Miss Podsnappery had insisted they were either little devils or didn't exist, but Cecelia had always known better. The Gnomes of the Stratosphere of Now were real and kind and they had come to deliver Cecelia and her father to the Land of Yesterday.

The Hungrig landscape grew closer and closer. Cecelia was almost on top of the balloon when the gnomes tossed a rope from the basket. Like a proper adventurer, Cecelia reached out as she passed, and caught it. She latched on and swung. The gnomes hoisted her up, and the hot-air balloon took to the sky.

Dropping into the balloon, Cecelia declared happily, "Father, I'm—"

Except her father wasn't there.

Cecelia rushed to the basket's rim. Close enough to the ground to see every house in Hungrig, she stared frantically over the edge searching for Widdendream. But in the place her house used to be, she found only a gaping hole with a dark lamppost alongside it. Her home was gone. Widdendream was the last house in the galaxy Cecelia ever thought would leave, as some did when the going got tough. But it had. The question was: Had her father escaped, or did Widdendream take him with it?

"Where's my father?" Cecelia bellowed over the hiss of fuel and winds. The gnomes raced back and forth. They avoided her clenched fists and heated stares while adjusting flames, winding gears, pulling levers, and retying ropes.

In a last-ditch effort to find Aubergine, Cecelia scanned the large basket's floor. She checked under blankets and boxes, behind four large propane tanks and two small jet packs, beneath the tangled vines of daisies—

Daisies?

Her hope sank. If the flowers *were* clues pointing the way back to her family as she'd thought, her father should be here. The certainty she'd felt earlier wavered. What if the daisies weren't clues at all, but more of evil Tuesday's tricks leading her even farther from her parents?

Cecelia cut a sly glare at the gnomes. What if they *were*

evil like Miss Podsnappery said? What if they picked Father up after he escaped and brought him someplace she'd never find him? Except they didn't look like tiny monsters from scary fairy tales; they were handsome in their small woolen hats, leather vests, linen pants, and strange shoes. And her instincts said she could trust them.

But . . . could she trust herself, when so many decisions she'd made in the past six weeks had ended up disastrous? Either way, if she wanted answers, she had to be smart and stay calm.

"Excuse me," Cecelia implored the gnomes rushing past her. "My father told me he'd be in your balloon. Do you know what's happened to him?"

They ignored her.

Cecelia's hair tried flagging them down, but they ignored it, too.

What was she going to do if she couldn't find him? How would she bring back her mother by herself? This would generally be the moment she burst into tears, but again, no tears came. Cecelia forced a smile, clasped her hands at her chest, and tried to sound persuasive. "Please, I'm begging you. Has my father been here?"

One of the gnomes—the one with smiling eyes and a big nose—paused for a beat and gave her the briefest nonchalant glance before attempting to sidle away.

Cecelia threw her calmness overboard, grabbed him by the back of his coat, and whirled him around to face her. "Hello," she said with a grin, hair writhing in the whipping wind. "My father, Aubergine Illustrium Dahl, have you seen him or not?"

The gnomes shared a brief and suspicious look before shaking their heads no.

Cecelia narrowed her eyes. They were definitely hiding something. Even the grumpy one with the long chin and impressive ears looked guilty.

Unacceptable.

"Okay, then, did you at least see my evil house pass by, or have any idea where it might have gone?" The kindly gnome nodded vigorously. Cecelia gasped with relief. "Oh, thank goodness! Can you tell me where you think it might be?"

From a secret drawer in the sidewall of the basket, the gnome with the kind smile pulled out a map—one like none she'd ever seen. He held it up to the surly-faced gnome, who hadn't stopped scowling since she'd come aboard. They appeared to agree on something and then showed her the map.

Cecelia inhaled an awed breath. Across the top half of the page, planets really spun, stars truly glittered, and nebulas actually swirled, all within a backdrop of black. A mountain range she'd recognize anywhere, which included a labeled likeness of Hungrig set between several tall peaks, ran along the bottom edge. The Stratosphere of Now—also labeled—comprised a glistening area right above the clouds, in the map's center. There was even a tiny rainbow hot-air balloon rising over the landscape, with an arrow pointing to it that read *You Are Here*. Snaking haphazardly though it all, from the bottom to the top, were three ghostly tunnels of silver. One occupied the upper section, another twisted through the middle, the last followed the base. Yet all connected to a giant black mass of mist on the right half of the map. Neither the black mist nor the tunnels were labeled. However, Cecelia had a sneaking suspicion the unlabeled channels were wormholes, and hidden within the shadow of smoke was the land she was searching for.

Cecelia regarded the curious gnomes, currently engrossed in scratching their ample behinds. "That giant black shadow on the map, that's the Haunted Galaxy, isn't it—the one said to hide the Land of Yesterday?"

The grumpy one shifted uncomfortably, while the other nodded in answer to her question.

"I knew it," she said. The friendly gnome tapped the center of the black mist; lightning stuck where he touched it. "Is that where you think my house is heading, with or without my father?"

The crotchety one twisted his lips and shook his head no. The sweeter one blinked up at her with sad eyes and seemed to want to say something.

"Please," Cecelia shouted at last, fists curled in frustration. "Would one of you just speak up and tell me what you know?"

The gnomes clutched hands and squished closer together, wincing under her gaze, but she stood her ground. Finally, the more agreeable of the two opened his mouth to answer Cecelia before the other could stop him. A torrential gust of wind left his lips and almost knocked Cecelia down. She clung to the basket's ropes, gaping at him with big eyes. The gnome clapped his hands over his mouth and the wind stopped at once.

"What in the world was that?" Cecelia peeled herself from the basket's back wall.

The pleasanter gnome hung his head in shame. The surly one smirked.

"Is that your *language*?"

One nodded. The other snickered. The balloon entered a thick layer of clouds. Perhaps this was what passed for Wordfartopotamus Syndrome in the outer atmosphere.

Evil Tuesday knew no bounds.

"I see. So, you can understand me, but I can't understand you?" The friendly gnome nodded again, eyes fixed to the floor; the bad-mannered one grinned even wider. Cecelia groaned. "Is there a way you can tell me your names, if you have a plan, or what you know of my situation?" One nodded and the other shook his head. Cecelia threw her hands in the air. "Can you tell me anything at all?"

The sweet one pressed his palms together as if in prayer and mouthed what looked like *please* to the grumpy one. A battle of waving hands and hats thrown to floor ensued. After the kind one stole the other's hat and threatened to drop it over the basket's edge, the grumpy one conceded and stepped forward. Head hung, he dug into his pocket and reluctantly handed her a sheet of glittery colored paper.

"Now we're getting somewhere, thank you." Cecelia unfolded the note.

Wild breezes ruffled the page. Fancily curled script ran up and down the letter, which read *To Whom It May Concern: Please read this note aloud.*

Cecelia cleared her throat and did as the note advised.

"Right. It says to please raise your hand if you are named Phantasmagoria?" Cecelia peered at the gnomes over the page. The happy gnome threw his hand high with excitement.

"Very good. Pleased to meet you, Phantasmagoria." Cecelia returned to the letter. "Next it says to bow if your name is Trystyng?" Mr. Cranky Pants, aka Trystyng, slid his hat off his head and bowed like a gentleman. Cecelia nodded and greeted him accordingly. "Hello, Trystyng. My name is Cecelia Andromeda Dahl, from Hungrig, a girl of eleven, who once resided happily at 2734 Saint-Exupéry Way and now exists in the depths of despair, permanently."

Trystyng farted.

Phantasmagoria hid his face in his hands.

Trystyng shrugged and then grinned.

Cecelia opened her mouth to say *How incredibly rude* when the strangest thing happened instead. The corners of her lips did this weird thing where they turned up especially high; her chin quivered, not with sadness either but with the kind of laughter that started slow and then exploded. Phantasmagoria's and Trystyng's green eyes popped big as lollipops as they erupted into a fit of giggle tears with her.

Laughing while her family was in danger made Cecelia feel guilty afterward, but for one shining moment, her worries, anger, and doubts had all melted away. She'd felt warm, as if the light from her lantern ran through her veins, and she wanted to hang on to that feeling. Cecelia hoped, sometime soon, to feel that warmth again.

The gnomes readjusted their hats and dried their laugh

tears. Cecelia set her eyes back on the letter. "Well, now that we've gotten that out of the way, let's see what other gnome facts we can find.

"The author goes on to state that this balloon is called the Dröm Ballong, which, loosely translated, means *Dream Balloon*. It also says that you're from the Stratosphere of Now, and that you each hold the title of Aeronaut, as well as the privileged job of navigating the Intergalactic Taxi to Yesterday."

Hope filled Cecelia. That map *did* lead to the Land of Yesterday. With their services, she would get her mother and father back for sure.

The gnomes pointed at the note.

Keep reading.

"Right. It says the operators of Dröm Ballong number nineteen, Phantasmagoria and Trystyng, have come to help the one reading this note find the answers they seek while navigating the perilous path to Yesterday in the safest way possible. Also, to help solve dilemmas that may or may not include the sudden appearance of cages in bodies, self-igniting and extinguishing lanterns, houses that switch from kind to evil, strange-language translation, evil-weekday possessions and how to stop them, crushing guilt, debilitating fear, and much, much more."

The last part consisted of such fine print she had to squint to read it, which caused her to speak extra fast. "Trystyng and Phantasmagoria may or may not be able to retrieve lost mothers, ghost brothers, housenapped fathers, or reform kindly houses that have gone over to the dark side." She glanced at them with worry.

They shrugged with an air of apology and tapped the note for her to continue.

The print on the next line was so small she needed to bring the paper to the tip of her nose to read it. "If passengers of Intergalactic Taxi number nineteen should find themselves stranded in space without a hope in the galaxy of being rescued"—she cut them a weary glance; they rolled their hands for her to go on—"said passengers would do well to remember this riddle and employ its answer forthwith: *What is an instrument of metal, man, and wind, and music to an Aeronaut's ears?*"

A strand of Cecelia's hair scratched her head as she continued. "Lastly and most important, the aforementioned gnomes may or may not turn into animals at any given time while entering forbidden lands, and under no circumstances are they to interfere with the process of those so filled with sadness, guilt, and regret that they turn themselves into—"

Smoke billowed up from the page. Cecelia dropped it with a scream as it burst into flames. Phantasmagoria quickly scooped it up and tossed it over the edge while Trystyng giggled inappropriately.

"Why did that happen?" She watched the flaming page drop into the clouds below. "I never got to finish the last sentence."

Trystyng hurried to the Dröm Ballong's edge and cheerily waved the letter goodbye. Phantasmagoria, with his back to his partner, opened his mouth to answer her question. Remembering the last time Phantasmagoria tried to speak and almost blew her overboard, Cecelia cried, "No! Never mind. Forget I asked." Phantasmagoria shut his mouth with a pout and Cecelia exhaled with relief. "No more talking, I think. That letter provided answers enough for now."

The Dröm Ballong sailed on a river of golden clouds. They were the exact shape and color of the lumpy pancakes her mother used to make every Saturday morning. Her father would flip them while telling bad jokes and Celadon poured too much syrup. Recalling these happy mornings caused Cecelia's heart to throb with a bottomless ache.

But this was no time for sadness or contemplation of lumpy pancake clouds. Cecelia had her family to save. "Pretending to be courageous is the first step on the road to *actual* bravery," her father once told her after a run-in with a ten-legged Burmese biting spider. Once, she had been fearless.

Maybe one day she could be again.

Standing at the Dröm Ballong's edge, far above the atmosphere, sunbeams arced outward in ten thousand shards of light. Cecelia tried to ignore the anxious look Trystyng and Phantasmagoria exchanged when they thought she wasn't watching. The sort of look one friend gave another when they knew something horrible was about to happen.

A look that said evil Tuesday wasn't done with her yet.

Chapter 10

THE BOY AND HIS SHEEP

Every night after her brother fell and broke, Cecelia jerked awake at one minute past midnight: the exact time of Celadon's fall. She'd bolt upright in bed to the same hideous *thud*. She'd tremble and gnaw her hair, and stare out the moony window as tears rolled down her cheeks. Then, after Cecelia had finally cried herself back to sleep, the nightmare that had been waiting would find her.

Within this dark dream, Cecelia woke inside a cemetery with a wrought-iron fence. A giant silver-blue moon hung low. She'd walk alone between the tombstones, each one bearing her name. Her long hair, the same shade as the midnight sky, blew wraithlike around her—as if each strand searched for someone Cecelia could not see.

87

"Hello?" she always called.

Ill winds whistled through trees in reply. Black clouds zippered the blue moon into darkness. White mists rose from the earth between graves and assumed a child's shape. Hundreds of ghosts wearing Celadon's face reached out to her with icy hands, clawing her dress, trying to drag her into the ground with them.

As Cecelia broke into a run, a blue ghost, identical to her, crawled from the meandering mists and knelt before a separate grave, one that bore her brother's name. "Help me," the phantom girl cried, holding out her unnatural hand.

But when she reached out to the ghost, it erupted into a colony of bats. Only then did Cecelia scream. Except the sound that exited her mouth was never a proper scream. It always came out as the hideous, deadly *THUD*.

This time, when she bolted upright out of her nightmare, she'd been running toward a brightly lit lantern twined with daisies, desperate to capture its light.

Cecelia found herself wedged between two snoring gnomes, one hand gripping her pen. She had left it in her pocket and was thankful she hadn't lost it along the way.

"Phantasmagoria, Trystyng, wake up." Their hats pulled over their faces, Trystyng farted like a slow trombone and Phantasmagoria snorted so loud, the balloon trembled. Cecelia's hair plugged her nose while she shook the sleeping gnomes. When she did, her middle crinkled ominously, across more of her than before.

Cecelia inspected her midsection before they woke. The perimeters of her paperness had increased dramatically. The parchment of her skin ran from the tops of her hips all the way over the base of her ribs. Oh souls. If her body papered completely, she would no longer be a living thing, and would be unable to deliver her letter, bring her mother home, or rescue her father. Who would save them then?

"Time is wasting, you two. Wake up." They responded with trumpeting snores. Cecelia rolled her eyes. "Wake up, *please*."

The *please* did it. The gnomes jerked awake.

Hats askew, they blinked at Cecelia, scanned the Dröm Ballong, and then sprang into action: checking maps, compasses, gas gauges, and jet-pack readings, and stowing the scraps of their last meal.

All the while, Cecelia stared out at the everywhere sky. She couldn't stop worrying—about her parents, Celadon, and Widdendream. Not even as the Dröm Ballong soared past nebulas close enough to touch. Not as Phantasmagoria and Trystyng shared a conversation in winds that nearly tossed her from the basket. Not even when they passed a blue planet inhabited solely by rabbits that winked and shouted "Hello there!" as Cecelia passed by. Not even as she wondered why people were so hard to understand when the language of animals seemed universal.

And then, out of the east, Cecelia spotted a red planet, which harbored a patch of healthy spring daisies.

Follow the daisies.

Even though the blooms she'd followed into the Sea of Tears hadn't led directly to her father as she had expected, a small something inside Cecelia felt the recurring daisies were important to finding her parents. That she could trust them, and they'd help her find her way home.

Just as Cecelia was about to ask the gnomes about the intriguing red planet, Phantasmagoria poked Trystyng hard in the chest. Trystyng whipped around and poked him back. Eyes bulging, nostrils flared in astonishment, Phantasmagoria jutted a finger at the propane tanks and threw his hands in the air. Trystyng mouthed, *Oh-oh.* Then smacked his palm to his forehead and threw Cecelia a rope.

"What?" Cecelia's hope plummeted. "What does that mean?"

Trystyng grimaced and pointed down. Phantasmagoria shook his head and gave Cecelia a look that said, *He's a mess, but he's our mess.* And without a second of warning, the fires that kept the balloon afloat sputtered and coughed and nearly died.

"Oh, I see," Cecelia said, holding tight to the rope. "We're going down."

The Dröm Ballong skittered and whirled and crashed to a landing alongside a dilapidated refueling station. Different-sized cylindrical propane tanks, in many states of rust and shine, lay scattered haphazardly among the endless red desert. Cecelia climbed from the basket and stepped onto the rippling sands. She checked beneath her sweater and assessed any damage. Her dress and self were dented and dinged but otherwise intact. Apart from skewed hats and rumpled clothes, Phantasmagoria and Trystyng seemed fine. They stayed behind to refuel the tanks, while Cecelia went to explore, as starlit space glittered overhead.

Hair bustling in every direction, thanks to the dry desert winds, Cecelia approached the daisies she'd spied from above. She stepped past pieces of scattered machinery poking from the rusty sands: metal bits and bolts, keys, corroded engines, plugs and cords in mad disarray. The wreck resembled the skeleton of a motorbike, but with wings. A royal purple blanket spread over the sand dunes alongside the smashed flying machine. Next to the blanket was a curious blond boy. A corral holding a midnight-blue sheep stood beside him. The boy was staring at her.

And the boy looked awfully familiar. . . .

Before Cecelia had learned to read, she used to sneak into Widdendream's dim library. It was one of those dark and mysterious rooms with too many upward shelves to count, rolling ladders, and comfy chairs. The sort of place you went to get lost, to climb inside someone else's dream and hide from annoying little brothers. One day, after a particularly horrific experience involving a spray hose and Celadon's dirty diaper, Cecelia discovered a story about an intergalactic explorer who liked to draw elephants inside snakes that looked like lumpy hats. The main character was a boy adventurer who wore a cape, befriended a fox, and loved the most beautiful red rose. Without understanding the words, Cecelia had felt like she understood the story from the pictures alone.

Something about *this* boy reminded her of *that* boy.

Cecelia approached the boy with yellow curls now crouched on his heels beside the sheep's pen. His inquisitive eyes followed every step she took. Eyes that said, *I have a secret and maybe you know it and maybe you don't, but either way, I'll never tell.*

At the last second, she decided to approach the sheep first. "Hello," Cecelia said. So far, she'd had good luck communicating with animals. Nevertheless, this one didn't even bother to look up. It just kept chomping daisies, ignoring her.

The boy giggled in hysterics beside her.

Cecelia moved closer to the sheep and tried again. "Hello, good sheep. Can you understand me?"

One bored sideways glance was all she got for her efforts until exactly one second later, when a question mark popped out of thin air over its head.

Cecelia narrowed her eyes at the troubling punctuation.

The yellow-haired boy laughed so hard he rolled onto his back and held his ribs until he cried. When he recovered from his fit of hilarity, the boy dusted himself off and approached Cecelia. "He's lived here his entire life," he said, drying his cheeks with one green shirtsleeve. "He only understands three things: eating flowers, this desert, and me."

Cecelia froze. "You understood me." She gaped at the boy, her eyes big as space. "I've been having some trouble communicating with others, and worried I wouldn't understand you either. But I do, and . . ." She peered harder into his sunny blue eyes. "Sorry, but you look so familiar. Do I know you from somewhere?"

The boy bubbled over into another round of laughing fits before forcing himself to be serious. "You could say I've been around, if that's what you mean. But him"—the boy aimed a thumb at the sheep—"he's never left this planet. It's his home. Together we run the refueling station. When we work together, we make a pretty good team."

"Hmm," Cecelia replied, patting the beast's wiry hair, the same shade as her own. "Does that mean you can understand him, then?"

"I couldn't at first." The boy scratched behind the sheep's twitching ears. "When we first got here, I had the prettiest rose in creation and I loved her deeply. The first chance my sheep got, he ate it." Cecelia cringed. The sheep chewed on without remorse. The boy continued. "I was hurt and sad and angry. For a while, I couldn't understand anyone or anything." *Wordfartopotamus strikes again.* "Still, I needed to understand why my sheep would do such a terrible thing. So I bravely studied his actions and reactions to the world around him. His habits and schedules, hopes and fears, until I understood everything about my sheep, including why he ate my rose."

"Then why did he do it?"

The boy glanced lovingly at his sheep. "He didn't know any better. It happened before our planet had daisies. I forgot to latch the gate to his pen, and in his hunger, he ate it." The boy sighed. "I do miss my rose. But she's not really gone. After I lost her, I started seeing her beauty in everything." He smiled knowingly at Cecelia. "I understand my sheep better because of my rose. I understand people better, too. In fact, I even understand why you're here."

Goose bumps arranged on her skin—paper and all. "You do?"

"Sure. You're on a quest for the mad house with the man trapped inside, and the woman who landed here that looked just like you."

Cecelia grabbed the front of his mint-green shirt and shook. "Yes! They're my parents and that's my house. Mother left for the Land of Yesterday to go after my ghost brother and now my house has turned evil and done terrible things—like almost certainly kidnapping my father and definitely trying to kill me—so any information you have about them would be greatly appreciated!"

Breath caught, Cecelia apologized for getting carried away.

"Completely understandable," the boy replied, straightening his shirt. "If I were you, I might have done the same thing. As for when the woman—"

"My mother."

"—your mother left, I can't say for sure. Time is funny here—it sort of *stretches*. Minutes roll on like hours, and hours like years, especially when heading toward the Land of Yesterday. I can tell you that her taxi stopped at our station to refuel a while back. I saw her and then she left. . . . Your house arrived not long ago to fill its gas burners." The boy leaned in close. Eyes twinkling with starlight, he whispered into her ear, "Your mother also asked if I could do something special for her."

Cecelia's pulse raced. "What?"

"She asked that if a girl with long midnight-blue hair stopped here, could I pass this on to her." He pulled something from his pocket and placed it in her hand.

"It's my mother's Joan of Arc action figure! I have one just like it. At least I did, until my house left with it, too. Thank you for keeping it for me."

Maybe Mother does *still love me,* Cecelia thought as her hair and heart danced for joy. She expected tears, but again, none came.

"You're welcome," the boy answered with a tinge of sadness, as if he'd just remembered the face of a dearly loved friend. "I lost someone once, a fellow adventurer who knew me better than anyone."

"Oh, I'm sorry," Cecelia replied. "Do you know where your someone went?"

The boy stared longingly upward, past the wind, sand, and stars. "I don't know. He flew away in his airplane one day and never came back. I've been watching the skies for him ever since."

Cecelia rested her hand on his. "I hope you find him, as

I hope to find my parents. I'll keep my eyes open for him on my journey, if you like."

"I'd appreciate that," the boy replied, back to his cheerful self.

Turning Mother's Joan action figure over in her hand, Cecelia thought of the day her mother found it. They'd been shopping in a tiny store in Hungrig called Myths of Milk, Honey, and Swords. Mazarine handed Cecelia a Joan figurine of her own and told her, "Remember this always: one girl can be fiercer than a thousand men and their king, the only one able to save them all."

Cecelia hoped her mother was right.

"You didn't happen to see which direction my evil house went, did you?" Cecelia asked the boy.

He hunkered back down beside his discombobulated motorbike and removed a rusted screw. "It went that way." He nudged his chin upward. Cecelia followed his gaze to a foreboding black planet with a blue moon. Something about it seemed familiar.

"What is that place?" Cecelia's hair thrashed like a wildcat in a trap. She stroked her panicking tresses, which refused to calm.

The boy dropped the broken screw with a clank and wiped his hands on a dirty cloth. His expression turned dark as the orb itself. "You don't want to know, trust me." The boy was a little too dismissive for Cecelia's liking.

"Oh, please, I insist."

He passed the sheep a handful of daisies. "Suit yourself. That's the Planet of Nightmares. It lures you to it by projecting the thing you want most. But when you land, it extracts your worst nightmares and then brings them to life." Cecelia's hair jumped onto her face like a flailing octopus. She pulled it free and tied it into a knot. The boy angled away from his sheep as if he didn't want it to overhear. "And, if you're not careful, the bad dreams root inside you and never let go."

"Who'd ever stop there if it's such a horrible place?"

"More than you'd think. Oftentimes, it's the ones who are saddest of all."

Cecelia faced the ominous orb. A white cloud passed close to its black surface and formed a perfect likeness of her mother, smiling and waving Cecelia forward. A feeling too strong to ignore overtook her—the feeling of absolute certainty.

What if her mother never actually made it to the Land of Yesterday? What if after giving the boy her Joan of Arc, the planet showed her Celadon and drew her in? What if Cecelia went all the way to the Land of Yesterday and her mother wasn't there but trapped in her worst nightmare, and Cecelia had passed her by?

Even if it meant jumping into her worst nightmare, she had to know for sure.

When Cecelia looked next, her mother's image had turned into her brother. His misty persona looked so real.

"Thank you for the warning, and for everything," she told the boy and his sheep. "I wish there was some way to properly thank you before I go."

A dry, gritty wind barreled toward them faster than they could run. It howled and whipped sand into the air, ripping daisies up by the roots. Cecelia and the boy covered their faces with their arms; the sheep buried its face in the sand. When the gust passed, it took most of the daisies with it.

The boy dusted himself off and shrugged. "You don't happen to have a miracle's worth of daisies, do you?" He laughed and dusted his sheep.

A miracle.

I wonder . . .

Cecelia caught sight of the gnomes. They waved frantically at her and then tapped their watches urgently. She gave them the signal for *I'll be right there.*

Then she removed her pen from her pocket while the boy watched with a half-cocked grin that reminded her of Celadon. Holding her pen high like a magician performing a trick, Cecelia unscrewed the cap, pointed it downward as if to write, and flicked it up and down three times. A few tears fell from the tip and melted into the desert. Wherever a teardrop landed, a patch of daisies bloomed.

"Will this do?" Cecelia smiled at the boy with a clever playfulness she hadn't felt since Celadon died.

"Yes!" The boy exploded with laughter and applause. An instant later, the question mark over the sheep's head disappeared. "See? You understand my sheep after all. This is exactly what he wanted. More daisies, he always says, and here you are, bringing him daisies!" The boy wrapped an arm around Cecelia and walked her back to the balloon. "I'm really glad you found us," he said. "I've done my share of traveling, and along the way I've found that unexpected miracles are what the journey's all about."

The gnomes appeared at her side, the balloon fired and ready.

"Guess it's time to go," Cecelia told the boy, who seemed like an old friend. "I hope one day we'll meet again."

The boy waved.

His sheep grunted what almost sounded like *bye-bye.*

"You know where to find us," the boy said. "Come back anytime!"

"I will." About to step into the balloon's basket, Cecelia turned to face him. "Wait, I never got your name."

"You know, it's been so long, I don't remember it. All that

matters is that I am your friend," he shouted over the wind. "And that I will always remember you!"

As Cecelia and the gnomes stepped into the Dröm Ballong, she shook an extra helping of tears from her pen. Daisies spread across the desert like a wildfire.

Cecelia heard the boy laughing as the balloon climbed into space.

Chapter 11

THE PLANET OF NIGHTMARES

"Trystyng, Phantasmagoria," Cecelia commanded, "I need you to land on that planet."

The gnomes frowned. When they craned their necks to see what planet she was pointing at, their eyes nearly popped from their knobby skulls. They tapped their watches and shook their heads with a hearty no.

Cecelia glared. "What do you mean, *no*? You're a taxi service, aren't you?"

Trystyng shrugged. Phantasmagoria rubbed his cheek and mulled something over. Struck with an idea, he gestured passionately at a pile of junk in the corner—spare fuel tanks, gnome-sized dinner jackets, books on dogs, way too many wheels of cheese, et cetera, then poked Trystyng, who twisted his lips into a scowl. After a brief deliberation, Trystyng reluctantly conceded to Cecelia's plan.

"Good. Then it's settled."

The gnomes shared another fussy glance and tapped their watches harder.

"I think I understand. You're on some type of schedule. I'll be as quick as I can, don't worry." She patted their shoulders, trying to look reassuring, even though her insides bubbled like hot sour soup. "Like my father says: pretending to be courageous is the first step on the road to actual bravery." She smiled with hope. "Maybe we can learn to be brave together."

The Planet of Nightmares hung as still as death in an infinite coffin of stars. And the closer they drew toward it, the rougher the cosmic seas became.

The winds howled and thrashed; Cecelia's paperness rippled in reply. The gnomes rushed to strap on their jet packs yet had none for Cecelia. Instead, they wrestled her into the only parachute left that hadn't blown overboard, which was two sizes too large. Comets shot at the balloon as if trying to push it back into space, like the heavens didn't want them to go. All the while, hurricane gusts attacked from all sides.

Cecelia's hold slipped. Half her hair wrapped around

the overhead bars, securing her before she blew away; the other half cocooned her head. Her parachute slid off in the fray. Unable to see anything but hair, Cecelia groped wildly. Finally, she latched onto a vine of daisies. But by the time she'd escaped her terrified tresses, the Dröm Ballong was spinning out of control and the gnomes were struggling to hold on.

"Trystyng! Phantasmagoriaaaaa!"

Cecelia propelled toward them, using the vine as an anchor. Her fingertips just brushed Phantasmagoria's, but he couldn't latch on. Trystyng gave her a look that said goodbye. A second later, her friends were sucked into space and she was left alone.

Cecelia barely had time to register their jet packs' flare to life in the distance before the Dröm Ballong hurtled toward the dark globe, and crashed with an echoing

BOOM.

Boom.

Boom.

Cecelia regained consciousness to her hair slapping her silly. She brushed it away and opened her eyes. A huge dead tree loomed over Cecelia like a monster's claw. It was night. Dim blue light covered everything. Cecelia experienced no physical pain, just a crushing resurgence of fear when she realized that the gnomes were really gone. Trystyng and Phantasmagoria hadn't wanted to come to this planet, but she'd insisted. Now they might be lost in space because of her.

Cecelia hugged herself tight. The gnomes were her friends. Not to mention her only way home.

In a panic, Cecelia checked her pocket: pen, letter, Mother's Joan of Arc—all still accounted for. She removed her Joan, held it before her, and whispered, "Please help me be strong," and then boldly scanned her surroundings.

She saw no sign of Widdendream or her mother. What if the planet had tricked Cecelia, but her mother hadn't been fooled? Still, the lantern flickered brightly within her. Something was here, waiting for her to find it.

Not far away, the Dröm Ballong lay tipped on its side. Its deflated rainbow corpse poked through low-lying mist. Leafless trees rose around her like the bones of dead witches' fingers. A dark forest loomed to her right. Blackened leaves and grass whipped from the left, making the same sounds her paper skin made when it crinkled.

When Cecelia opened her sweater to check her parchment middle for damage, she found her paperness had started inching toward her back.

Surprisingly, that wasn't her main concern.

A watchful blue moon hung low, illuminating the rolling

mists and dreadful silence. A chill of ice ran up her spine.
Everything looked familiar in a very bad way.

"I know this place."

Her scalp tingled and breath seized.

"No."

The sour scent of rotting and dampness and newly dug
graves licked her skin.

"Anywhere but here . . ."

In the months before Celadon's passing, he used to wake
in the middle of the night and tiptoe into Cecelia's bedroom.
After his nightmares of broken houses and falling and not
waking up, he would lift her covers and crawl into bed beside
her. Cecelia would stir when his arctic toes poked at her legs.
Still, she never kicked him out. He helped keep her warm on
especially cold nights, which Cecelia found quite useful. And,
though she would never admit it, she also found it comfort-
ing. Then evil Tuesday came and he was gone and her own
nightmares began.

Now here she was in the graveyard from her bad dreams,
with no one to comfort her but herself.

Cecelia sprang up and ran for the forest. Hair trailing in a
widow's veil, she leaped over scattered bones and dead stumps
with roots that tried to grab her. Restless spirits seeped out of
the ground, calling to her as she passed:

"It's so nice down below, Cecelia."

"No murderous houses here!"

"Come, paper girl, I know just what to do with you."

Out of breath, Cecelia paused at the edge of the forest. Everything had gotten too loud and ugly too fast. She needed to think. But how could she, surrounded by all this death? While racking her brain trying to figure out what to do, the terrible stench of rancid greenery draped her like a wet sheet. One heart pound later, a sound wound out of the woods.

Bang, Bang, BANG.

Thud, Thud, THUD.

Widdendream.

Footsteps like dynamite sped toward her. Trees uprooted and flung for the moon. Her evil house barreled out of the woods on tree trunk legs and splaying root feet. Its arms of broken boards and walls swung at its sides, while its horrible candlelit attic eyes flickered in anger. It shook the planet off its axis with each thundering step.

The monster stopped in front of her.

Cecelia looked it dead in the eyes.

"CECELIA DAHL," Widdendream hollered, so loud she had to cover her ears. "You should not have come without Mazarine. Until you bring her to me, your father is mine!" The second-floor balcony curved into a black-toothed grin.

"And because of your insolence, I must do something else to hurt him. Or maybe I'll just hurt you instead."

Whip fast, Widdendream's huge, hard paper arms reached back and uprooted a large dead oak, then hurled the tree at Cecelia. She dashed sideways. The tree crashed into the mist and shook the black earth. Cecelia coughed on splinters and dust. Her heart flapped in her chest like a rabid bat, but she held her ground. "I didn't come here for you, Widdendream. But now that I'm here, I demand to know if Father's all right, and to warn *you* that if you don't stop hurting him, I won't do as you've asked." She raised her chin and puffed her chest. "I'll even tell Mother what you've done to him. Then she'll never want to come home to you!"

Widdendream shook like a rain-wet dog. "You wouldn't dare." Moths and dust, old photos of Mother, and paper snowflakes belched out with Widdendream's fury.

She grinned. "Watch me."

Widdendream paused. Its face fell in confusion. Cecelia thought she glimpsed something else (regret? shame?) in its expression. But a second later, it was back to its arrogant and malicious self, stomping the ground with a savage roar. Bits of its brokenness spewed out between its cracks, showering Cecelia in debris.

"Run!" Aubergine shouted from the attic. "Leave this

place while you still can." The sound of her father pounding the walls ripped Cecelia's spirit in two.

"Widdendream, stop!" Cecelia yelled.

"No," her house sneered, more ruthless than ever.

A few old photos of her mother lay strewn on the ground. In each, she looked so happy. Now her father was kidnapped and her mother may be in trouble. Cecelia wanted her family back, more than anything.

Blood boiling with rage, Cecelia rushed at the house, kicking and punching Widdendream's door. "Leave him alone! My father never did anything to you. It's me you want to punish, so punish me and let him go!"

The front door burst outward and threw Cecelia straight back. Black vines rolled out like a tongue. She landed hard and skidded on her behind.

"Leave here. Bring Mazarine back to me. Fail this task," Widdendream roared through the open door, "and you will never see your father again!"

The sudden sound of rustling wings filled the air. Red-eyed bats by the thousands flew out the front door in a gust. They smacked her face and tangled in her hair. They dived under her sweater and squirmed. She unbuttoned her sweater, flipped onto her belly, and crawled out from under the swarm, until she and her hair had room to fight back.

Tresses and fists flying, Cecelia and her hair chased the demonic bats into the night.

Hunched over and gasping, Cecelia could still feel leathery wings and bladed claws scraping her neck. Her hair wouldn't stop shaking. Yet, unlike in her nightmare, when the bats defeated her, this time *she'd* conquered *them*. Cecelia couldn't help feeling proud. She may not have been successful in rescuing her father—yet—but if she could beat the bats, maybe that meant she could beat Widdendream, too.

Cecelia shouted toward the attic, "I'll get you out, Father. I swear it!"

Widdendream straightened its slumped shoulders and drew up to its full height. "Hurry, paper girl, before I do something you'll regret. And remember," it growled, "I'll be watching you." The drapes in the attic windows pushed shut. Its black tongue of vines drew in. The forest dimmed. Her house lumbered back into the woods, with her father still trapped inside. Widdendream may have won this round, but Cecelia vowed she would save her parents or succumb to full paperness trying.

Cecelia hurried toward the balloon. If she was going to leave this nightmare, she needed to get the Dröm Ballong operational. When she was younger, she'd spent countless hours in the Dahl basement assisting her father with his fantastic array of inventions—gadgets that ticked and whirred, buzzed and flew, exploded and blasted off, though she'd never tinkered with any on her own. Still, she had Joan. And if Joan of Arc, a farm girl from a small town in a big world, could ask King Charles VII for an army and get it, then she, Cecelia, from the small town of Hungrig in an equally big world, could gather the courage and determination needed to fix this broken balloon.

Cecelia worked for what felt like hours, trying everything she could think of to fix it: setting it straight, maneuvering the rainbow silk, pulling this lever, twisting that gear, turning gas valves left and then right, re-and-rechecking fuel levels (the tanks were still half full). After flipping the basket over for the hundredth time, something popped on her paper skin, like a button flying off a sweater.

Oh souls.

Faint light spilled from her middle. She looked down. The rusted door of her cage had broken through her paper doors, leaving Cecelia open and frayed at the edges. A sudden wind roared up like a monster, whipping sand hard enough to sting. Each time her dress began stitching itself back together, her cage door caught in a gust and ripped her open once more.

Frustrated with every last thing, Cecelia squeezed her eyes tight, threw her arms and head back, and screamed into the wind, "If this is a nightmare, I'm ready to wake up!"

Swift heat burst forth from her middle. It spread through her body by degrees, along with a powerful uprising of light. The last time her lantern had burned so clear and bright, Celadon had appeared.

Excitement bounced through her cage like a bell that would echo forever.

Under the howl of the wind, Cecelia heard clothing flapping behind her—the snap of a velour jacket Cecelia would recognize anywhere.

Chapter 12

HE LOVED HIS SISTER MOST OF ALL

Cecelia sprang up and spun around so fast, she nearly tripped and fell on her face.

Wavering before her, wearing ghostly sneakers and a weary expression, was her brother, dead but not all-the-way gone.

"Celadon?" Cecelia cried. "Oh souls! What's happened to you?" He looked terrible. He'd become so transparent, she could barely see him.

Swaying like a slow pendulum, Celadon reached for his sister with misty green hands. He gasped, "Help me," and slipped silent as a cloud to the cold dead earth.

Cecelia bent over to help him. Her cage swung open with

a shrill creak, spilling bright lemon-colored shadows every-where. She slapped the stupid door shut, but it wouldn't stay closed. "Why are you here and not in Yesterday?"

Celadon parted his eyelids. His pupils glowed. Each word looked painful to speak. "I tried. Didn't make it. I passed here while being dragged back to Yesterday. Heard Father shouting . . . saw Widdendream, and fought to get away."

Cecelia clenched into a knot.

Widdendream.

He wheezed, "I'd gotten so thin the pull of Yesterday couldn't hold me. It dropped me, and I landed here." A pale-green tear rolled down Celadon's cheek like a miniature crystal ball. Cecelia wiped it away. "I followed Father's voice, in case I could help him escape. But my energy was too drained. I stayed away too long, and I was too weak to help him." He looked away, ashamed. "Now I'm too weak to help you. I've failed you. I'm sorry, Cee-Cee."

"Celadon, no. None of this is your fault." Cecelia cupped his face in her palms. A sudden tingling numbness swept up her left arm. A warning bell chimed in her head, which Cecelia promptly ignored. "Don't worry. I'm going to save you. We'll escape this nightmare together, you'll see."

He may have been barely visible, but Cecelia could still see him smiling. "I always knew you were a hero. Glad you're finally starting to see it." Celadon choked; his eyes bulged as he gasped for air. "I might know a way out of here . . . a secret passageway to the entrance to Yesterday." Wheezing, he glanced sideways into the thickening mist. "It's buried, over there . . . at the root of my own worst nightmare." Cecelia tracked his gaze, but all she saw were dead trees, wastelands, and mist.

Dueling winds bombarded them from all sides. Cecelia's cage crashed open and shut, tearing her apart once more.

"You'll never make it with that broken cage," her brother whispered. Celadon reached into the wind with the palest green hands and used the last of his strength to fix her. Cage relocked, he collapsed with exhaustion. "Good as new."

With the broken door of herself closed, her paper section of dress was finally able to seal. Chin trembling, Cecelia found a sad smile and gave it to him. "Thank you, little brother. Now I demand you stop fading this instant so I can get you out of here."

Cecelia moved to scoop him up.

"It's too late. I'm almost gone. Once I disappear all the way, I won't even stay alive as a ghost."

The air quieted. Every crinkle of Cecelia's paperness amplified. Mist rolled in from all sides, thick as water ready to drown the world.

"I won't let that happen." Hair flying high, Cecelia lifted her brother's body of pale-green mist as easily as if he were made of feathers. "I'm getting you out of here—*now.*"

Her fading brother made no reply.

Cecelia ran. Soft and sultry mist curled her ankles like long pale-blue cats. The very air seemed to purr. She searched for the secret passageway that, moments ago, Celadon had told her was buried at the root of his worst nightmare. She recalled his old night terrors from when he was alive: darkness, blue moon, monster, a shove from behind, falling and not waking up.

Her steps faltered. She'd forgotten that part of his dream. *"Something pushes me and then I fall,"* he'd said. Strange, how that was so like the way he'd actually died.

Head buzzing, arm numb, the ghost of her brother blinking in and out of sight in her arms, a familiar iron fence poked out of the mist. Her breath turned to granite in her lungs. She moved through the graveyard gate knowing all too well what she'd find: a replica of the cemetery where her brother was buried—his worst nightmare as well as her own.

The blue moon dimmed. Foul winds whistled through the bones of giant deceased trees. Tombs, old and moldy, rose from the fog like ancient broken teeth. Unlike the real cemetery in Hungrig, each gravestone in this haunted place bore the same words:

"Oh souls, that can't be good."

Black clouds closed the moon in sudden darkness. Ribbons of dreadful green mists rose from the earth between graves and assumed a girl's shape.

"Celadon, wake up."

Hundreds of ghosts, each wearing Cecelia's face, reached for her with icy hands, clawing her dress, trying to drag her into the earth with them.

"Celadon."

Cecelia hurried to find the hidden entrance to Yesterday, but she wasn't sure where to look.

"Celadon, wake up!"

It was so dark, and her brother so sheer, she could barely see him at all. His eyes remained closed, their glow gone. Cecelia was running out of time.

Ghouls with long, writhing hair ripped at her skirt, sweater, and boots. She ran faster, and thought harder about the clues Celadon gave her. He said the entrance sprang from his worst nightmare. And if this was a replica of his cemetery, and he said the entrance was here, then maybe his worst nightmare was dying.

If it was, then she needed to find Celadon's grave.

The instant she thought this, more than half of the specters pawing at her body burst into balls of light and vanished.

Those that remained came on even stronger, howling and growling, whispering things as she passed.

"Nobody likes you, Cecelia."

"Not even you *likes you."*

"You're terrible!"

"Selfish."

"Worthless—"

"Go AWAY!" Cecelia kicked the nasty liars until they smashed into fizzling dots of light.

"Cee-Cee," her brother wheezed, and cracked open his eyes. "I'm going . . ."

"Hang on," Cecelia cried, entering the last row of graves. "Almost there!"

Blood pumping wildly, Cecelia sprinted up the aisle. The faster she went the quicker the ghouls on her heels exploded like hideous gems. At the very last grave, Cecelia skidded in her tracks. The sight of it sent a familiar icicle through her heart.

"Oh, Celadon," she whispered. "It's yours."

Cecelia knelt before the finely carved cross, so beautiful and horrible she wanted to cry. Her knees sank into the loosely piled soil beneath her. Dead vines and daisies twined the stone.

Follow the daisies.

This had to be it.

Gently, she placed Celadon's ghost beside her. He appeared sheer as a mirage, only a glimmer in the corner of her eye. She pushed the vines aside to reveal writing hidden on the cross beneath.

HERE LIES

THE BODY OF

CELADON IGNATIUS DAHL.

BORN HAPPY,

DIED WITH

NO REGRETS.

LOVED

HIS SISTER

MOST OF ALL

Celadon's funeral came rushing back. She remembered how it had occurred on a Tuesday that wept gray tears from heaven. How storm clouds chilled Hungrig to the bone and the preacher wore a cassock, black as her heart. That no one in attendance used an umbrella. How Father said it was because they were rejoicing in their ability to still feel rain. How her little brother had been buried with his favorite things: a plush cat he carried everywhere, two carved wooden dogs, and two paper dolls—one pale green like his eyes, and another midnight blue like Cecelia's. She laid them both on his chest before they lowered him into the cold hard ground.

And now here he lay, fading into oblivion, and here she was again, hovering over his ghost. *You're the only one with the power to help him, so do it.*

Cecelia raced to put together the clues that would lead to the Land of Yesterday:

1. The entrance was hidden.

2. It was buried at the root of Celadon's worst nightmare.

She glanced down at the fresh earth beneath her. If his worst nightmare was his death, the root had to be—

That's it.

Using her hands, Cecelia dug deep into the soft soil until she hit open air.

"Celadon!" She dug faster and faster until the rabbit-hole duct lay exposed. "I found it!"

Ugly green fog had covered Celadon's body while she'd been digging. Cecelia reached in to scoop him up. But she couldn't feel him.

"Celadon?"

Fear gripping her bones, Cecelia ran her palms over the ground, but couldn't find him.

"CELADON!"

A wild wind rose: parting the clouds, returning the moon, and clearing the mist.

Horror struck as Cecelia lowered her eyes. A green paper doll, almost identical to the one she'd placed in Celadon's coffin during his funeral, lay in his body's place. She lifted the paper doll and held it under the moon's light. "Celadon?"

I'm so sorry. Forgive me. . . . Then her gaze dropped onto her hands.

She rolled up her left set of sleeves. Her arm had turned to midnight-blue paper, same as the skin of her abdomen and sides.

Cecelia held her paper brother over her heart and screamed into the wicked black wind—for her parents and her brother and herself.

From deep within the dark woods, Widdendream laughed, cutting her cries short.

Cecelia gritted her teeth. "You."

Blood on fire, lips curled into a sneer, lantern blazing through her paperness, Cecelia faced the forest. Her hair flying upward in a rogue gale, she held Celadon's paper body high, and shouted into the moonlight, "I WILL TAKE YOU DOWN, WIDDENDREAM, IF IT'S THE LAST THING I DO!"

And from the darkness came a burst of light.

Chapter 13

THE HAUNTED GALAXY

From the center of the dark woods came an explosion of light. Cecelia swung around, caught in Widdendream's glow. The monstrous house leaped skyward from the skeletal trees. With the flaming jets of a rocket, it blasted into the atmosphere. The higher it rose, the more it tilted and bucked like a mad bull. It struggled, gas burners sputtering, yet managed to set itself straight. Widdendream's laughter echoed and died in the cradle of stars as it finally dipped out of sight.

Cecelia glanced down at her brother, reduced to a paper doll. Jaw clenched, hair thrashing in the sideways wind, she fought against her anger. Darkness fell upon her, crashing down in shards of black glass.

But Cecelia would not shatter with it.

Dropping to her knees before Celadon's grave, Cecelia steadied her breathing. Bit by bit, her jaw unclenched and pulse slowed. She opened the doors above her navel with her free hand and unlocked the clasp of her cage. Then Cecelia tucked Celadon safely inside, alongside her heart.

His Celadonness radiated through her—his scent, spirit, laughter, and his unique fingerprint of life. Her lantern flared with a brighter, more brilliant shine. *"I'm never all-the-way gone, Cee-Cee,"* he had told her when she first returned from Yesterday. *"No matter where I am, I'm never far from you."* She hadn't fully grasped his meaning at first, but now she understood.

Cecelia closed her cage. Thanks to him it was as good as new. Her paper skin and dress threaded back together and sealed instantly. "I'll see you again, Celadon. I promise." Without looking back, Cecelia slid her boots into the secret passageway beneath her brother's grave, wriggled inside, and let go.

The drop wasn't far. She landed on her feet inside a dimly lit tunnel. The hole closed over her head. Cecelia inhaled slowly with awe and followed the trail of light to the end.

The short cylindrical passageway resembled a giant drainpipe that ended abruptly in the center of space. Emptiness below and above her, Cecelia stood at the tunnel's edge. Pearled cobwebs hung from star to star in gauzy nets. The air wailed like possessed souls. Cecelia patted her shivering hair while tarnished watches frozen in time, wedding rings with bony fingers still attached, and swarms of lost baby teeth drifted by. This space seemed hidden from the rest of the cosmos, and felt haunted, forgotten. Sad.

Cecelia leaned out of the drainpipe tunnel and called into the black jar of stars, "Hello?"

Not a single thing answered back.

At her voice, a metallic sign materialized before her. In misted script, it read:

> *To all those living, BEWARE.*
> *Go no farther. Turn back now.*
> *For this is the way of the lost,*
> *of death, and wandering ghosts.*
> *Leave Yesterday in the past, Traveler,*
> *lest ye become a lost thing yourself.*

Now she knew what this lost space was. She'd read all about it. This was the Haunted Galaxy surrounding the Land of Yesterday; this was the shadowy glob riddled with wormholes on Trystyng and Phantasmagoria's map! After everything she'd been through, she was almost there.

No time to worry about any posted sign's ominous

warning, she needed to figure out how to get from the end of this tunnel into Yesterday.

She wished the gnomes were here.

Dangling her legs over the precipice of everywhere and nowhere at all, the Dröm Ballong's rules sprang to mind: *If passengers of Intergalactic Taxi number nineteen should find themselves stranded in space without a hope in the galaxy of being rescued, said passengers would do well to remember this riddle and employ its answer forthwith:*

What is an instrument of metal, man, and wind, and music to an Aeronaut's ears?

The riddle.

That's it!

But what was the answer? Cecelia's hair scratched her head. If she didn't solve that riddle, she was sure to end up a paper doll like her brother, an autumn leaf tossed about in a whistling wind, and who would save—

Wait.

Wind was part of the riddle. What was an instrument of metal, man, *and wind*, and music to an Aeronaut's ears? She pondered and thought for seconds and minutes and what felt like numerous eternities until the answer appeared.

Whistling! A whistle is an instrument of metal, man, and wind. Taxi drivers did seem to enjoy whistling, didn't they?

She wasn't sure if a whistle would be music to an Aeronaut's ears, but she would soon find out.

Perched on the precipice between now and Yesterday, Cecelia dug her miraculous pen from her pocket and carefully took it apart. She placed each section of her pen, except for the outer canister, back into her sweater pocket, then allowed herself a smile. Next, Cecelia raised the hollow outer tube to her lips and blew the loudest whistle she'd ever created—so powerful, it echoed through space.

Cecelia held her breath.

She waited.

The cobwebbed stars and ghosts and black nothingness quieted to dust. Celestial glitter whirled into the tunnel, glazing Cecelia in black and white specks of shimmer. Then finally, in the distance, a familiar hum filled each particle of matter in perpetual space.

Could it be?

A colossal shadow arose before her, lifting as fast as Cecelia's triumph.

It is!

Inch by inch the silhouette drew higher until she was positively certain. Miracles upon miracles, she'd solved the Aeronauts' riddle, and Trystyng and Phantasmagoria had heard her call. A new Dröm Ballong, identical to the other that crashed, appeared. Slathered in glitter and stardust, Cecelia screwed her pen back together, returned it to her pocket, and jumped into the Dröm Ballong's basket.

"Phantasmagoria!" Cecelia kissed his pink gnome cheeks.

"Trystyng!" She planted a smooch on his forehead, despite his resistance, and grinned when he blushed.

"You have no idea how happy I am to see you." Both were so coated in cobwebs, they looked like tubes of gray cotton candy, but Cecelia hugged them anyway.

The Dröm Ballong rose into the cold casket of stars. She looked at them and asked earnestly, "You won't leave me again, will you?" Phantasmagoria placed his hand over hers, patting reassuringly, and opened his mouth to speak.

"No!" Cecelia splayed her hand in his face. "Never mind, I don't need to be blown awa—"

A small asteroid struck the basket and knocked Cecelia off balance. Without warning, her right leg went numb; a spark of worry lit as her leg folded beneath her. The gnomes jumped in and guided her safely to the floor.

"Trystyng, Phantasmagoria?" The trio stared at her leg: it had become midnight-blue paper, same as her arm had. The closer she drew to the Land of Yesterday, the more of her flesh she seemed to lose. Not only that, but the whole of her black-and-gray dress had papered along the way, too. Her striped paper skirt ruffled in the breeze. With Trystyng and Phantas-magoria's help, Cecelia pushed awkwardly to her feet.

Holding steady to the basket's rim like the Pirate Queen of the Haunted Galaxy, she proclaimed to the outer reaches of haunted space, "Tuesday remains treacherous and wicked. But we will not let that stop us, will we, boys?" Trystyng and Phantasmagoria shook their heads and broke into an impromptu jig.

A snap later, they pulled Cecelia in with them.

"Oh, now, wait just a minute—"

The gnomes grabbed her hands. Holding her up, they spun her around the basket. Cloaked in webs of gray, glitter everywhere, they danced and shrieked with laughter. In that moment, despite her paper skin, Cecelia felt free. Trystyng and Phantasmagoria had become her friends. And she knew right then that, no matter what, they would never let her fall.

Northern lights, otherwise known as aurora borealis, cracked through the hoary darkness before them. Phan-tasmagoria's and Trystyng's eyes bulged like grapes at the sight. They nodded to each other and passed Cecelia a vine-clustered rope to hang on to, then left her side.

"What's this for?" she asked, having flashbacks of crash-ing and seeing them sail off into the cosmos.

Hang on, Trystyng mimed.

A vacuuming whoosh preceded a flash of green. The

dancing lights absorbed the balloon into a chute of warm green flames. The gnomes rushed about madly. Cecelia clasped tight to the basket's edge and peered down the glowing green chute. As she did, the Dröm Ballong dropped like an unhooked elevator toward a black desert below.

A black desert. Like the one in the Land of Yesterday.

"We're heading to the Land of Yesterday, aren't we?" Cecelia shouted to the gnomes. Her hair rippled like blue fire over her head.

They paused from their frantic hurry and nodded gravely back.

All at once, daisy vines unwrapped from the basket and spun Cecelia in a protective cocoon. The gnomes covered her body with theirs. And within the strange cocoon of flowers, friends, and space, memories of yesterday bombarded Cecelia. How, after Celadon died, she barely spoke, ever, to anyone. Because everything she said came out wrong. For a while, she turned to her pen and paper for a cure to her tongue's clumsiness—easier to let the paper take the blame, fold her feelings into an envelope and give them away, than to say the wrong thing or keep her emotions locked inside. She thought about how she pushed away her friend Bram, with whom she'd once held hands, and shared her wildest, most secret dreams.

These memories danced around her and carried the weight of the sky.

She remembered what her mother told her after the funeral for her hamster, Professor Rick Von Strange. "Cecelia, do you know why you're so special?" her mother had asked. Cecelia shook her head as her hair dried her tears. "You saw in him what few are able to see in another. You saw yourself within him. Each time you looked into his eyes, you saw your own happiness, love, vulnerability, and pain. You're a rare child to be able to see so deeply inside the heart of love. . . ."

More than anything, as the Dröm Ballong plunged through the green cyclone of lights, Cecelia remembered how for days after Celadon's death she longed for her mother to comfort her like that again, to understand how she felt, to understand her. She needed her mother to tell her everything would be okay, that Celadon's death wasn't her fault. But her mother couldn't do that. Because she was too busy drowning inside her own tears to help anyone else.

Then, as fast as they'd come, the fog of memories let go and the Dröm Ballong crashed.

Yesterday had arrived at last.

Cecelia crawled from the wreckage into the whirling black sands with her mother's tears still firmly in mind. She decided she wouldn't drown like her mother had.

Cecelia decided she wanted to swim.

THE CATERWAUL OF THE LAND OF YESTERDAY

Cecelia's ears rang with the quietest quiet. Her hair floated north, reaching for the faraway stars. The night skies no longer seemed haunted. Thanks to the daisy cocoon, and Trystyng and Phantasmagoria's protection, Cecelia's paper limbs and torso had not been damaged in the crash. A white sickle moon loomed overhead, coating everything in a glow of mystery.

In the distance, an old English-style castle stood alone on the windy horizon. Four tall and thin towers, twisting like licorice spires, rose toward strange constellations; flags snapped from each peak, all bearing a griffin clutching a snake eating its own tail. It glowed like a radioactive beast at the horizon's edge. The castle's stone shimmered in shades of mazarine and lit the black sand like neon. Stars clustered around the turrets and seemed to be whispering, *Come, Cecelia, come* . . .

Her mother had to be inside.

Cecelia scanned the black wastes for the gnomes. The hot-air balloon lay crumpled in the shadows to her right. Directly beside it, two small still shapes had collapsed in the sand. Trystyng and Phantasmagoria!

When Cecelia readied to race toward them, an explosion burst from the crash site. Cecelia blew backward. Fire shot into the sky. The Dröm Ballong's basket, half buried in a drift of black sand, billowed with flames.

Without a second thought about her paperness, Cecelia sprang to her feet and ran as fast as her parchment leg would allow toward the inferno. Trystyng and Phantasmagoria leaped up and dashed toward her, shouting in the blustery way they did, as the Dröm Ballong blazed behind them. The trio met in the middle and crashed into a hug.

"Are you all right?" Cecelia asked while brushing debris from their vests.

Both nodded. Trystyng licked his fingers and extinguished a burning thread on Phantasmagoria's hat. Phantasmagoria hugged Trystyng extra tight. To Cecelia's surprise, Trystyng smiled sweetly. They seemed as vigorous and wonderful as ever.

"Good. Because you'll need to be in tip-top shape to navigate the castle. I've read about it. Amytheria Nox, the famous warrior hermit of Mount G, wrote in her book, *Guardians of Legend and Lore*, that this fortress, known as the Castle of Never More and Once Again, was the most perilous castle in the Multiverse. I never knew if it was real until now, but there it is." The gnomes rubbed their hands together, entranced. "Amytheria stated the fortress itself would do anything to trap the living within its walls and steal all their tomorrows."

The gnomes gave Cecelia thumbs-ups.

Scared, but undeterred, she nodded. "Let's go."

Finally, she would see her mother. She would hand her the letter, written with her miraculous pen filled with her equally miraculous tears, and gain her forgiveness for her part in Celadon's death. Her mother would know how to handle Widdendream and rescue her father, and they would be a together family once more. Cecelia warmed at the thought, but her happiness faded fast.

Lost and forgotten things littered the glittering onyx desert. Cecelia stepped over each object with care. A cracked locket lay at her feet, holding black-and-white photos of sweethearts inside. Farther ahead, a toy truck, with more scratch than paint, bearing the inscription *Serena the Great!* lay half buried in sand. Next, a tattered suit and a wedding dress spilled out of an ancient trunk, along with a handful of books. Another step and a once white teddy bear (*Sand Goon*, according to its tag) gaped up at Cecelia with its remaining eye. *"I'm lost,"* it seemed to say. *"Have you seen my boy?"* She grimaced as she stepped over a stack of unopened letters bound by a frayed red ribbon, addressed *To Mom, with love.* They reminded her of the unread letter to her own mother in her pocket, and that sometimes letters remain forever unread.

A tawny flash of light popped out of the sand by her feet, scurried up her leg and onto her shoulder. "Professor Rick, it's you!" Cecelia patted her hamster's ghost. He placed his paw in her hand like he used to. "I'll never forget you," she whispered in his ear. One nose wiggle later, he scampered back into Yesterday.

Another shape bloomed from the night sands to her left. A full-size fighter jet with a white star on one wing protruded like a dark desert rose. Cecelia's pulse leaped at the words written beneath the circled white star: *To the boy and his sheep. I looked with my heart and found what I was looking for. Your friend, A. 1st August, 1944.*

Cecelia's heart clenched. The boy with the sheep mentioned he'd lost a friend—one that had flown away and never returned. Cecelia felt responsible for the message, and vowed to keep it safe for the boy, as he'd kept her mother's for her.

A roar of wind blew, and with it came her mother's voice. It sang out from the direction of the castle: the lullaby Mazarine used to sing to Cecelia and Celadon to lull them to sleep. So lost was Cecelia in her thoughts and the song, she hadn't noticed the thundering footfalls shaking the sands behind her until it was too late.

Trystyng and Phantasmagoria sprinted ahead. Mouths wide and screaming with tornado-force winds, they tried to grab Cecelia's hands as they passed, but Cecelia couldn't hang on. She fell to her knees. The gnomes skidded to a halt and ran back for her, just as Cecelia turned.

A towering feline beast stopped a few paces away and loomed over them. Standing on its hind legs, it was the height of a maple tree. Cecelia had to tilt her head all the way back to see the great cat's face. Its whiskers, longer than Cecelia's arms, rippled in the breeze. Its fangs gleamed in the moonlight. Silver-and-charcoal fur covered its body. An unpromising growl emanated from its throat.

This must be the Caterwaul, Guardian to the Land of Yesterday.

She'd heard stories of the Cat Guardian, each more terrifying than the last. And yet, observing it now, with its fuzzy face and long whiskers, chubby belly and sorrowful stare, Cecelia struggled to feel afraid. Maybe all this paperness had withered her fear as it had her tears. Maybe that second wish she'd made had started to come true—that she could be heroic like the explorers on her walls and in her books, like she used to be.

"Hello, fierce and terrible Guardian," Cecelia said, bowing to the Caterwaul. "Is that your castle over there?"

The gnomes looked at her like she'd lost her marbles.

"Yeeesssss," the Caterwaul growled. It lowered its massive head and moved an arm's length from Cecelia face. She saw herself reflected in its shimmery eyes. *"Thiiisss siiiide of Yesss-terrr-daaayyy is miiiiiiinne."*

Cecelia grinned and clapped her hands. "You can talk! And I understood you!" Her face fell as she turned to the gnomes. "I guess that means the Caterwaul has lost loved ones, too."

Phantasmagoria and Trystyng were too busy yanking the Caterwaul's fur and kicking its toes in an attempt to divert its attention from their girl to respond.

The Caterwaul, paying no notice to the gnomes' efforts, stepped back, extended one upturned paw in front of Cecelia's face, and yelled *"GIIIIIIIFT!"* so loudly, the desert lifted around it in a whirl.

She'd forgotten the Caterwaul demanded a gift as payment to stay in Yesterday and ate those who came unprepared. Also, anyone who stayed too long in its desert became trapped inside here for eternity.

No pressure.

"GIIIIIIIFT!" the Caterwaul repeated, lips rippling from its roar. Anyone in his or her right mind should have groveled, but not Cecelia. For she glimpsed behind the Guardian's eyes a secret wish only she could grant.

On instinct, Cecelia lunged forward and hugged the beast tight. Her paper middle crunched. Her hair wrapped its body and snuggled merrily into its fur. The Caterwaul wailed hard enough to shatter the stars, yet did not pull away. Instead, it lifted her into its mammoth arms, held her with love, and very quietly, so only Cecelia could hear, the Caterwaul laughed.

Cecelia crawled up and onto its shoulder and whispered into its tufted ear, "I have the perfect gift for you."

Cecelia burrowed into her sweater pocket and produced her finest gift. She held it up to the Caterwaul. "I do hope my special pen will suffice as payment for my visit to your castle, Caterwaul of Yesterday." She didn't relish the thought of letting her pen go, especially since it might contain the last tears she would ever cry. Still, the giant demanded a gift, and this felt like the right one to give.

The Caterwaul either grimaced or grinned or was about to eat someone alive by the look on its face as it received her pen. Then, slowly, carefully, the Guardian set Cecelia back down on the sand.

Cecelia stood before it and bit her lip.

Her hair went absolutely bonkers with anticipation.

The gnomes jumped in front of Cecelia and braced for attack.

The Caterwaul watched them in stunned silence for a moment before its whiskers quivered, lower lip shook, and eyes swelled with delight. Finally, the Caterwaul fell backward with a grand *plomp* and burst into a laughing fit. When it finished rolling about in the sand, it wiped its eyes and groaned in its grisliest voice, *"Thaaank yoooouuuuu."* The Caterwaul's breath hit her with the scent of spring daisies and perfumed the desert night.

Daisies.

A small grin spread through her.

She was on the right track.

"One daaaaay," the Caterwaul groaned as it straightened to its full height, *"I wiiillll repay giiiiifffft."* Tears glistened on the short fur beneath its eyes. It brushed Cecelia's cheek with the soft parts of its paw. *"III wiiilll dryyyyy yooourrr teeears aaand heeeellp Ceceeeliaaa baaack hoooommme."*

Nodding, Cecelia answered, "Deal."

The three followed the Caterwaul through the wasteland of forgotten treasures, toward the castle. Along the way, Cecelia thought again of the dangers of Yesterday. How the castle would do anything to trap unwelcome visitors inside.

As the castle loomed ominously before them, Cecelia's hair curled around her neck and turned as cold as ice. "There, there," Cecelia whispered, stroking her panicked blue locks. "With the Caterwaul as our Guardian, nothing bad will happen. That cat wouldn't hurt a fly."

Chapter 15

MOTHER, IS THAT YOU?

At six years old, Cecelia fell off her bicycle. Her leg had shredded so badly, her tears didn't stop for what felt like an age. "Tears have a power," her mother had said. "When they come forward, you mustn't try to stop them."

Cecelia searched her mother's kind eyes and asked, "Why not?"

"No matter what language a person speaks, how old they are, where they come from, or what they've been taught, tears are the one thing everyone understands." Mazarine caught a teardrop at her daughter's chin and held it up to the light.

Then her mother did something that Cecelia hadn't understood at the time. She placed Cecelia's tear on her tongue, where it vanished without a trace. "Your pain is my pain. If we ever become separated and have trouble finding our way back together, shed a few of these, and I will find you."

Or, Cecelia thought, grasping her letter of tears on her approach to Never More Castle, *I will find you.*

The Caterwaul led the way to the bastion at the horizon's edge. Sand grated Cecelia's eyes. Her hair rode the maelstrom of wind gusting from all points of the compass. The gnomes fought to stay upright in the torrent of black grit. Then, without warning, the desert jerked as if it was a rug yanked out from under their feet.

Cecelia, Phantasmagoria, and Trystyng flew into the air, cartwheeled, and dropped to the ground. The Caterwaul rode the rolling sands with ease.

"Caterwaul," Cecelia shouted. "What's happening?"

Objects popped out of the desert around them like coffins from flooded graves: old rocking chairs, swing sets, photo albums, jewelry boxes, love letters, strands of clipped hair. Everywhere they looked, memories of lost time blocked their way.

The Caterwaul, about twenty paces ahead, faced them, stretched its jaws, and roared, *"Desert angreeeey with Caterwauuuul. Doessss nooot want Mazariiiine to goooooo."*

Cecelia dug in her heels. Her mother was definitely here, and not even the Guardian of Yesterday would stop her. "I'm sorry, but that's unacceptable. One way or another, I'm getting inside that castle and taking my mother with me."

The desert rolled and pitched, and screamed. The Caterwaul howled out a hurricane. *"Muuust nooot enterrrr!"* It tried desperately to hand Cecelia back her pen. *"Pleeeease,"* it moaned quieter, *"the miiiists aaaarre awaaaaake."*

Cecelia braced against the desert's fury. "I'm not sure what you mean about waking mists, and I'm sorry your desert is upset, but I must find my mother." Her hair whipped about in outrage. "Please step aside, Caterwaul. My friends and I intend to pass."

Trystyng and Phantasmagoria shook their heads at each other, shrugged, and finally nodded emphatically, ending their silent conversation. The wind shrieked like an injured animal all around them.

"Yeeesterdaaay doesn't let anyyyone goooo!" The Caterwaul, looking panicked, pointed at something behind Cecelia's back. *"Noooow, it coooomes fooor yooooouuuu."*

Cecelia turned around. A tidal wave of swirling sands rolled toward them at an alarming speed. The sky blackened to pitch.

Sandstorm.

"Run!" Cecelia shouted to the gnomes over the squall and made a break for the castle.

More objects rose from the desert to stop them. She leaped over each and only fell once. The gnomes couldn't keep up. Cecelia feared Trystyng and Phantasmagoria would become lost to the storm until they shared the fastest glance/nod/mischievous-grin combination ever. A micro split second later, the gnomes morphed into dogs.

Dogs!

Cecelia stared at them in astonishment. Phantasmagoria, now a silvery German schnauzer, and Trystyng, a snaggle-toothed bulldog, dashed forward and stood before Cecelia, growling at the Caterwaul blocking their way.

She recalled the disclaimer in the Aeronaut's note, the one that went up in flames, which read, *Lastly and most important, the aforementioned gnomes may or may not turn into animals at any given time while entering forbidden lands. . . .*

Phantasmagoria nudged Cecelia's leg. His eyes seemed to say, *What're you waiting for? This is our chance. Let's roll!* Cecelia wanted to hug them, kiss them, and ask them a million questions, but now certainly wasn't the time.

Trystyng and Phantasmagoria nipped and snapped at the Caterwaul's ginormous feet until it danced clumsily out of the way. Cecelia sprinted after the gnomes, Joan of Arc clenched

in one fist, with these words held firmly in mind:

I am not afraid. My heart is true. I was born to do this.

Out of nowhere, a rogue black wave knocked her head over heels. Cecelia flew into the air and landed with a *rip* and a *shred*. Her right ankle of midnight-blue parchment severed almost in half. She registered no pain, but didn't think she could walk.

The dog-gnomes barked in unison, trading glances between her and the storm. It was coming fast. For a moment, she thought her ankie might mend as the doors of her middle had, but no such luck. She needed to wrap her ankle so she could run—if only she had something to hold it together.

A section of her hair, harder and coarser than she remembered it, ruffled forward, volunteering as sacrifice. Fisting the strand of coarse locks, she pulled. They came free too easily, and soon, she knew why. Each strand was flat and wide and dry. "Paper," Cecelia said. She checked the remainder of her frantic hair, but the rest had yet to parchmentify.

The gnomes barked. The winds grew so violent, she could barely sit straight. The dog-gnomes kept bouncing away, and the Caterwaul was nowhere in sight.

Regardless, Cecelia knew what had to be done. She wrapped her broken ankle in lengths of blue paper hair. Ignoring her fast-growing paperness, Cecelia crisscrossed it around her foot and up her leg like a Grecian sandal and tucked the ends in place. Without looking back, she ran and didn't stop until she arrived.

Up close, the castle shone like a polished gem. Mazarine-colored mist ribboned out through the open castle doors. The long wooden drawbridge had been lowered, likely by the Caterwaul, who was waiting for them inside.

A moat circled the towering castle. As the trio crossed the bridge, Cecelia noticed the moat wasn't filled with water but flowed with thousands of what looked to be lost paper souls. Each human-size cutout was thin as a sheet and had big, hollow black eyes. They undulated past in eerie silence. Some had slender black lines for mouths; others had razor-sharp teeth; some stared straight at her. They floated, layer upon layer, too creepy to be alive. Cecelia shivered at the thought of ending up like them.

Once over the bridge, her inner lantern flamed brighter, warmer, filling her with reassuring light. *Mother's in there. I can feel her.* Cecelia took a deep breath and peered in through the door. Then she glanced down at the gnomes. "Are you ready?"

They nodded and appeared as calm as tea with the queen.

"I am, too." Cecelia smiled bravely, focused on how far she'd come instead of her wobbly stomach, and then stepped inside.

Purple-blue mist snaked the floors in the foyer of Never

More and Once Again. Everything here reminded her of her mother. Mazarine's voice drifted toward her, humming the lullaby she'd heard earlier in the desert. Maybe Cecelia's mother felt her presence and called to her now?

Cecelia grew so preoccupied with her mother's voice she didn't notice the purple-blue mist wrapping her neck like strangling hands.

"Mother?"

She didn't notice the castle doors slam quickly behind her, locking Trystyng and Phantasmagoria outside. Nor did she hear the haunted *THUD-THUD-THUD* of her brother's fall replayed in the walls like a drum as she shadowed the mists up the staircase. Cecelia didn't register that Yesterday's castle resembled Widdendream exactly—right down to the broken knob on the top of the banister.

In a trance, Cecelia followed the mist and her mother's lullaby, unaware that with each step another strand of her hair dried to paper. By the time she reached the end of the second-floor corridor, all her hair had crisped and dried. Yet her heart continued to flutter in a flesh-and-blood flurry of happiness as she arrived at her mother's bedroom door.

Cecelia ran her palm over the familiar entrance. Without looking back, she whispered, "Phantasmagoria, Trystyng, we made it."

As she grasped the doorknob, Cecelia got the distinct impression that she'd forgotten something, but couldn't think of what. Haunting music wound through the halls. Cecelia began to feel sleepy.

"Mother," she said with a yawn. "Is that you?"

Mazarine stopped singing. Mist leaked like poison gas from the walls.

"Ah, Cecelia, my love, I'm so glad you're finally here."

Chapter 16

NOTHING WILL MAKE ME FORGET

The moment Cecelia entered the bedroom, she felt completely at ease. The purple-blue mist blended into the purple-blue curtains, into the bedspread on her parents' bed, the paint of their dresser, and the circular rug in the middle of the floor. Soft music hummed from each molecule of air, songs sung by her mother when she was small. The deeper Cecelia immersed herself in the castle, the dimmer her lantern became, and the faster reality slipped away.

Cecelia blinked. Her sleepiness grew into a lazy euphoria while she stared at Mazarine, who sat at her vanity brushing her long midnight-blue hair.

Mazarine smiled at Cecelia in the mirror. "Hello, my darling."

"Mother!" Cecelia rushed to her side. "I've been searching everywhere for you."

Mazarine turned in her seat and embraced her daughter. "Look no further, here I am." She held Cecelia at arm's length and inspected her crown to toe. "So," she said, clapping her hands together, "it's a brand-new Yesterday. What shall we do, hmm?"

Cecelia wrinkled her brow. *A brand-new yesterday.* She'd never heard that one before. Although she guessed she liked the sound of it.

"Anything," Cecelia said with a delirious grin. Purple-blue mists swam around her like curious fish. "I'm happy with whatever you want to do."

The picturesque Hungrig countryside rolled on outside the window: gentle green hills, snowcapped mountains, puffy white clouds, spring breezes, rustling leaves. The purple-blue curtains billowed like ghosts. A twinge of not-rightness squirmed in Cecelia's belly. Like the view should be something different, something darker, deader, black-sandier. But as soon as the mist rolled thicker across the bedroom floor, and the music hummed a bit louder, she forgot all about that pesky not-right twinge.

"Wonderful. Ah," her mother chirped. "I know. Let's gather our little family, just you, your father, and me, and go on a picnic. What do you say?" Mazarine's eyes flashed. "It will be just like old times."

A picnic? That didn't seem possible for some reason—but why not?

An abrupt cloak of dense clouds, the same shade as her mother's eyes, blotted out the view of Hungrig. Cecelia watched the fog spin in a hypnotic dance. And suddenly, a picnic sounded completely possible, and like a perfectly wonderful idea.

"Yes," Cecelia answered, each eye blinking out of sequence. "That sounds delightful."

"Then it's settled." Mazarine swiveled back to her mirror. "Run along and get changed. Your father should be home soon."

While Cecelia watched her mother brushing her long, silky hair, an image bombarded her memory: of a boy with black hair and pale-green eyes. He used to sit on her rug and watch Cecelia as *she* brushed *her* hair. And oh, how her hair had loved the attention. A few strands always swam out behind her and tickled the boy.

The boy. Her brother.

Yes.

Except the photographs on these bedroom walls contained only her mother, father, and Cecelia, when they should have shown the boy, too. She didn't understand. She remembered him so clearly.

Celadon.

"Mother?" Cecelia asked before leaving. "Where's Celadon? Should I tell him to get ready for the picnic, too?"

Mazarine stopped brushing midstroke. Her face hardened in the mirror. A cold embrace of air clamped around them as if the room had sealed their bodies in ice. "I'm sorry, sweetheart, who?"

A fresh wave of mists glided toward Cecelia from all corners of the room. Mazarine held up her hand; the vapors halted immediately.

Were the mists listening to her?

"Celadon, my brother."

Mazarine turned in a slow arc and locked eyes with Cecelia. Her expression shot flaming daggers into her soul. "If this is a game, I don't like it. You do not have a brother. You said it yourself: *I wish I never had a brother.'* I believe those were your exact yesterday words?" Her eyes sparkled merrily as she turned back to the mirror. Mazarine's voice poured as smoothly as warm crème from her lips: "Yesterday gives us a chance to forget the pain of today, Cecelia. You'd do well to remember that. Now be a good girl and get dressed for the picnic. This is a day for fun."

Mazarine waved her hand, and the mists were on Cecelia once more.

Drowsily, Cecelia mimicked her mother's words, "Be a good girl, get dressed, this is a day for fun," and left the bedroom, more bewildered than ever.

In the hallway, the lullaby music grew fainter and less magnetic. A memory nagged at Cecelia as she gazed across the hall. She recalled a door. And a boy who once lived behind it. When she pictured the boy, the lingering mists cleared.

I have a brother.

Cecelia grinned with his memory. Black hair, pale-green eyes, light and joy in his smile. Cecelia closed her eyelids. In the darkness, she saw Celadon plain as ever. Her father told her once, *"No force anywhere is greater than love."* Cecelia fought to hold on to this truth.

A small table beneath the window at the turn of the staircase held a vase brimming with fresh daisies. On instinct, Cecelia picked one for Celadon.

Daisies, that meant something, didn't it?

Moving forward, she glimpsed the staircase banister. A nightmare flashed in her mind—of a boy and a fall and a death, and an angry, murderous house. She couldn't tell if those things happened or if they were a bad dream.

Glancing over her shoulders, making sure her mother's door remained closed, Cecelia knocked on the door of the boy she couldn't forget. *"You do not have a brother,"* her mother had said. But she remembered him. And if he didn't exist, this door wouldn't exist either, right?

"Celadon?" Excitement bubbled through her, but she kept her voice low. Her paper hair wouldn't stop squirming. Cecelia waited and then pressed her ear to the wood. The room remained dead quiet. After another moment, she opened the door.

Darkness, as deep and sticky as tar, filled the room. "Hello?"

When Cecelia reached into the void with her paper hand, the darkness, the door, and the room shattered into a million crystal shards that fell without sound.

Heart thundering like a stampede of wildebeests, Cecelia gaped at the now blank wall. "Celadon," she whispered, and placed one hand over her lantern. "No matter where I am, I'm never far from you."

A hand clamped down on her shoulder.

Mother.

She shoved the daisy into her pocket and turned.

"What are you up to, Cecelia?" Mazarine loomed over

her, seeming taller than she had before. Colored mists wafted through her grin of teeth. "I told you to get ready for the picnic."

"Oh, I thought, um, I heard something odd. But it was . . . nothing." Cecelia put on her best smile. "I'll just go change." *I have a brother. He lived. And then,* she thought sadly, *he died.*

Nothing will make me forget.

"There's no room for strange here," her mother said, grabbing Cecelia's sweater sleeve. The hem tore off in her hand. Mists poured through the cracks in the walls and floors. Lullaby music returned, louder than before. "When in doubt, listen to the mists. They will keep you happy and safe."

Cecelia had to fight to control her obnoxious hair, which kept thrusting toward her mother. "I understand."

"Wonderful. And, on second thought, I think you look fine the way you are. No need to change."

Cecelia glanced down at her ripped sleeve, hiding her frown. "Whatever you say."

"Don't forget to smile, Cecelia. You know how your father loves it when you smile." Mazarine clasped her right hand. The instant their palms touched, Cecelia's skin prickled and crackled and numbed. Her arm papered in a wave to her shoulder.

Oh souls.

"Something wrong, Cecelia?" her mother asked innocently as mists wound about Cecelia like eels and slipped into her mouth and nose.

"Nothing at all," Cecelia answered, trying not to breathe. "Everything's fine."

"Excellent." Her mother paused on the stairs. She glared at her daughter's lantern as it struggled to stay alive. "But do be careful, Cecelia. Yesterday must be cold and numb to be safe. Paper children with stubborn inner fires almost always get burned."

As Mazarine led Cecelia downstairs, Cecelia struggled to remember her paper brother lying in a cage by her heart. She wanted to think that the hope scrabbling inside her had claws, feathers, and teeth, and was willing to scratch, rise, and bite to survive. She fought to feel the fire of life within her and the power she possessed to shine. Cecelia resisted until the mists won.

The castle would not go down without a fight.

SLIPPERY, CRUMPLY THINGS

Mazarine wore a purplish-blue sundress and sandals, both matching her eyes exactly. Her blue hair floated around her shoulders of its own volition. The picnic basket was almost packed. So far, it contained everything Cecelia loved best: French toast with oodles of syrup, peanut-butter-and-blackberry-jam sandwiches, garlic-stuffed olives, and cheesecake. The only thing left to pack was her absolute favorite—pie.

"Are you ready for telling stories and laughing by the lake?" her mother asked, seeming almost normal. "It's a perfect day for a family picnic, don't you think?" Mazarine kissed both of Cecelia's cheeks.

Her lips felt hard and flat. Like paper.

Cecelia tried to focus on her mother's question, but a procession of vivid images kept marching through her mind: of Celadon, gnomes, hot-air balloons, black deserts, lit lanterns, and a sea of daisies. The sense that this place wasn't her real home poked her in the gut, yet she couldn't get it all straight in her head.

"Cecelia? Are you listening?"

"Hmm?" Cecelia replied, eyeballing the mists. "Oh, right. Yes. The perfect day for a picnic." The streamers of colored smoke drew back with satisfaction, and so did the hypnotic tune. Cecelia forced an especially bright smile.

"That's my girl. Now gather your blue sweater. The mists around the lake can get chilly."

Cecelia peered out the kitchen window. She should have seen mountains and a lake encircled by daisies, but now there was only thick silver-green fog.

"Greetings, Dahl family," said Aubergine, breezing into the kitchen. He wore a casual shirt, the same deep plum shade as his name, and pants to match. "Is everyone ready to gorge themselves on sandwiches and pie?"

Cecelia's heart leaped at the sight of him. She couldn't remember *why* exactly, but she felt like she hadn't seen him in ages. In her excitement, she forgot to remember any odd details about this place, and hurried over to hug him like she'd never let go.

"Well, that's quite a reception. I love you, too, Cecelia." He knelt down to speak with her face-to-face. Looking deep into his eyes, Cecelia could see right through them, past the green, into black. "We can live happily here, you know," he said, no longer sounding like her father, but a slippery, crumply thing. "Everything's always wonderful inside the mists of Yesterday."

A flash of memory seized her brain. Of her father, trapped in Widdendream's attic, screaming her name.

Her lantern pulsed, and then, it blazed.

Cecelia backed away slowly. Her father kept changing shape. One blink and he looked like one of those paper spirits she saw in the moat: flat body, black eyes, and sharp teeth. Two blinks later, her loving father would return.

"What's wrong, Cee-Cee?" Aubergine asked. Reddish-purplish mist seeped from his eyes, nose, and mouth. "Aren't you going to get your sweater like your mother told you to?"

Her breath stopped. He called her Cee-Cee. The only person who called her that was her brother.

Celadon.

Cecelia glanced at her mother, who was currently glaring at her father, and then narrowed her eyes at them both.

"Nobody calls me Cee-Cee but—"

"Now, now, Cecelia," Mazarine said. "You're just excited about our outing." The woman who may or may not be her mother stopped cutting the pie. She circled the kitchen island and approached Cecelia, knife still in hand. Cherry pulp dripped from the blade in gruesome strings. Mazarine cradled Cecelia's face in her hands—knife and all.

"In this perfectly brotherless Yesterday, we can have daily picnics, just the three of us. Free of sadness, grief, and those dreadful things called tears. We can stay just like this, where nothing bad ever happens. Nothing dangerous, nothing new, the same yesterday lived again, and again, and again."

Sticky warm drops of cherry dripped onto Cecelia's forehead.

"And again, and again," her father chimed in. Not as Aubergine, but the tall, thin, fully formed, black-eyed, sharp-toothed paper doll. "Soon you'll understand that the mists are *good*." He pushed in beside Mazarine, wiped the cherry from Cecelia's forehead, then ate it. "We'll have so much fun. You'll realize that having no brother is better than having a dead one—especially when you're the reason he died."

Cecelia's hair writhed in rage. "That's not true! What happened was an accident. And I *do* have a brother. And even though I lost him, I don't want him erased from my memory, my life, or my heart. He was real! I love him, and I won't let the last of him go!"

Aubergine growled, "We are your parents, and if we are to have a tear-free yesterday, that boy *cannot exist*." Colored mists oozed from their skin. The mists wound about Cecelia like hungry anacondas and attempted to seep into her pores.

"The mists are good, Cecelia," Mazarine said with swirling hypnotized eyes. "They take away all the pain, just like that."

The doorway that led to the hall was only two feet to her right. Cecelia eyed it carefully. "Get away from me," she said, and took a step for the door.

In a flash of unbelievable speed, the Father thing clamped down on her paper arms. "Don't leave us, Cecelia." He pushed his face into hers. "We love you more than life itself."

"Cecelia." Her mother, now the same monstrous thing as the father, wrapped a midnight-blue sweater around Cecelia, forced it onto her, and then hugged her—tight. "Soon you'll be a lightless paper thing, like us."

Peering over the Mother thing's shoulder, a splash of color Cecelia hadn't seen earlier grabbed her attention from the hall. The daisy she had plucked from the vase lay on the floor. It must have slipped from her pocket. Familiar words chimed through her brain: *Follow the daisies.*

The mists thinned even more at the mantra of daisies. And Cecelia's jumbled memories fell into place. This was not Widdendream. They were not her family. This was not her home. She was inside the Castle of Never More and Once Again—a place that wanted to trap her in its walls and steal all her tomorrows.

She had to escape from these foul paper things.

As fast as she could, Cecelia ducked out of the Mother thing's embrace. She darted for the hall, paper parents hot on her trail. Mists scourged the corridor like a raging river. Yet the harder she focused on daisies, the more the mists, and her mind, cleared.

The Father thing called through the fog as Cecelia thumped up the staircase. "Cee-Cee, we don't want to be late for the picnic. Come back like a good paper girl."

He was close behind.

The Mother thing grabbed Cecelia's hair; a clump ripped out in her grasp. "Come back, Cecelia," the Mother thing crooned in her lullaby voice. "I'll love you like an only child, the way you've always wanted."

"You're wrong!" Cecelia snapped, sprinting ahead. "It's better to have loved someone than to never have had the chance to love them at all."

The Father thing grabbed Cecelia's flesh ankle and squeezed. Numbness washed up her leg from toes to hip, trailed by a rumpling crunch. Her left leg had succumbed to paperness, too. The paper devil grinned up at Cecelia with sharp parchment teeth, and then laughed, as her hair fought the beast to get her free.

Cecelia focused on her brother and on how somewhere her parents still needed her. Thoughts of them weakened the mists and music even more. The Father thing hissed and let go of her leg. All at once, the house she mistook as Widdendream lost its glamour and revealed its true form.

She wasn't running up Widdendream's staircase, and these weren't Widdendream's walls. The dark medieval stairwell of Yesterday's castle appeared. Torches perched on musty walls. Paper rats scurried past her boots as she ran. The parental creatures scuttled like venomous spiders up the ancient stone steps, hissing Cecelia's name.

Daisy in hand, Cecelia followed her intuition, her memory, and her light to the location she first mistook as her mother's bedroom, and threw open the door.

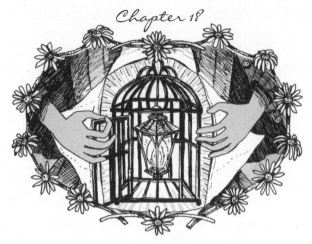

Chapter 18

A PRISONER AND A DARING ESCAPE

Cecelia slammed the heavy wooden door behind her and locked it. The evil Mother and Father things were right behind her. Holding the handle, Cecelia felt it jiggle, twist, and then turn. She heard them breathing behind the door with paper-bag lungs and gripped the handle harder. Her parchment hands kept slipping over the circular knob.

Maybe if she couldn't get a good grip, they couldn't either.

The walls were hand-cut stone. Torches lined the room; firelight blazed from iron sconces; shadows loomed long and wicked. What at first had appeared as Widdendream must have been a trick of the mist.

Cecelia's gaze fell. She'd been so focused on the paper

devils trying to snatch her she hadn't noticed how her light had grown. Or how, since entering this room, it glowed like a mazarine sunrise through her dark paper skin. Colored mists leaked in from under the crack in the door. They snaked her body, drawn to her light, trying to extinguish it for good. She'd been able to fight them off earlier, but didn't want to take any chances.

Wrestling off the extra sweater the Mother thing forced onto her, Cecelia rolled it up and laid it across the base of the ancient-looking wood door to stop the leak. The sweater seemed to be working.

Still facing the door, the scent of rain and daisies and her mother's perfume circled Cecelia. She paused to inhale the sweet scent. When a noise, more like a whimper, echoed from the back of the room, Cecelia swung around at once. A cage, identical to the one inside Cecelia's body but tall as the ceiling, held someone who looked like her true mother captive inside.

"Mother?" Cecelia sprinted to the cage. "Is it really you?"

Mazarine's eyes were closed. Her body hunched on the floor. She wore her favorite gray dress, the one she had on the morning she left for the Land of Yesterday, and her best tall boots. Midnight-blue hair swayed about her shoulders in a nonexistent breeze. She wasn't the same mother Cecelia remembered. Much of her skin had turned as blue and hollow as Cecelia's, and her dress had papered, too. From what she could see, everything but her mother's neck, legs, and boots had transformed.

"Mother, it's me, Cecelia."

Mazarine didn't move so much as an eyelash.

Slithering and shuffling sounds eked in from the hall. Cecelia glared at the door. Yesterday's minions weren't going to claim her or her mother, not if she had anything to do with it.

Cecelia tugged on the cage's heart-shaped padlock, but it wouldn't budge. She thought maybe she could flatten herself out enough to squeeze through the bars, but her own cage made doing so impossible. Cecelia twisted the lock, kicked it, and punched it, until finally her hair intervened. It picked the lock easy-peasy, and Cecelia slipped inside.

"Mother?" Cecelia knelt beside Mazarine. Her skin looked as rough and dry as sand, yet, even still, she retained her beautiful glow. Up close Cecelia realized her mother's eyes had papered, too. "Are you awake? Please tell me you're okay."

Mazarine's eyelids fluttered like a raven's wings. She raised her head in a slow arc, and said with a sigh, "Oh, Cecelia. My beautiful girl." Cecelia wanted to cry. It really was her. She tried to speak, but no words came. "I knew you'd come for me."

Outside the castle, wind gusted past all and everything. Grains of sand whipped the window glass like countless granular hammers as Cecelia helped her mother sit up, and kept one eye on the door.

"What happened? Why are you locked in this cage?" Cecelia rested a palm on her cheek—she felt so cold. Like a no-mittens, midwinter's-night cold. "How did you turn into paper?"

Mazarine shook her head. "The mists lured me into the castle. One of them pretended to be Celadon. Like a fool, I believed it and followed it into this cage." Chin wavering, Mazarine stifled a cry. "Then it trapped me. I cried so hard, and for so long, time seemed to stop. Soon, I'd turned into this. Your father would have known better."

Distressed as her mother was, Cecelia decided not to mention her father's kidnapping, or Widdendream's madness. Or that Celadon had died a second time and what remained of his paper body lay housed in a cage near her heart. However, there was one thing she needed to do without delay.

"Mother, before anything else happens, I need to give you something." Cecelia touched the letter for her mother still tucked inside her pocket.

"Of course." Mazarine straightened up.

Cecelia inhaled a deep breath, and placed the letter in her mother's hands. "I wrote this for you with the special pen you gave me. The one you said was—"

"Powerful enough to bring writer and reader together, when combined with the ink of the heart," Mazarine said fondly. "I remember."

"After you left, I thought that if I wrote you a letter with my saddest tears and you read it, it would bring us back together, like magic. Then you'd understand how sorry I was for everything I'd done, all the hurt I caused our family."

Mazarine accepted her daughter's letter of tears and put on a brave smile. "No, it's me who should be sorry. I was so lost in grief. It was as if half my heart had crumbled to dust. I didn't know how to act, what to feel, how to move forward. I couldn't find myself. I became obsessed with getting Celadon back, but not once did I blame you." Mazarine stroked Cecelia's hair. "Don't you know? I would have done the same for you."

Heat pinched the backs of Cecelia's eyes. "I thought you hated me for what happened to Celadon. I thought you blamed me like I blamed myself. I worried you might never forgive me."

"Now you listen to me, Cecelia Andromeda Dahl. There

is nothing to forgive. I love you more than anything in this world or the next, the same way I do Celadon—with a love like a wild horse with no hope of being tamed. I told you as much in the letter I wrote you. Didn't you read it?" Mazarine held up the envelope Cecelia had given her moments ago. "I figured you had, since I got yours."

Cecelia's eyes bugged. "What? You *did* get my letter? The one I sent before I left home? You got it and wrote back and that's why my letter looks different?"

"That's right. The Caterwaul, which you must have met, caught it in the desert."

The Caterwaul.

"The Cat Guardian found your letter, opened it, and told me it had never read a more moving plea. But because the Law of Yesterday prohibits it from releasing those who came here of their own free will, all he could do to help was give me your letter and enough time to write you back. I explained everything in the letter I wrote you, the one you're holding now." Mazarine's hair wrapped Cecelia in paper ribbons. "I hope one day you can forgive me."

Cecelia ripped open the strange little crystalline envelope colored in the shade of tears and eagerly read her mother's words. The note was long, and heartfelt, and more beautiful than Cecelia could have ever imagined. However, the loveliest line she'd ever read in her life was this: *My dearest Cecelia, you are the heart that beats alongside my heart. No matter where I am, I am never far from you.*

The heat behind Cecelia's eyes doubled, tripled, quadrupled, and suddenly, a series of midnight-blue gems plunked to the stone floor. They were translucent and hard as diamonds. She caught a few in her hands.

Her heart twisted at the truth of them.

"I'm . . . crying." Cecelia's laughter bounced off the walls. "The last tears I cried were the ones in my letter to you." She laughed harder. "I thought I never wanted to cry again, but it feels good, really, really, good."

Mazarine gave her a sorrowful smile. "I'm sorry for leaving you, Cecelia. I just couldn't let Celadon go. And because of that, I put us both at risk. This is my fault."

"No. It's not." Cecelia took her mother's hands. "You didn't know this would happen. That makes this an accident, and they aren't anyone's fault. That's why they're called accidents."

"Thank you, sweetheart. But I'm not as strong as you are." Tears balancing on her lower lids, Mazarine squeezed Cecelia's hands. "It seems your wisdom has eclipsed my own."

"How about, just for now, I'll be strong for you?" Cecelia replied. "Being there for each other is what families do, right?"

Sparkling, crystal-like tears, identical to Cecelia's, bounced off Mazarine's cheeks. "Yes, that's right."

Cecelia hugged her mother again, wanting to take away her pain. Though, deep down, she knew all she could do was be there for her, if and when her mother needed her.

The torches on the walls sparked. Stale air knit around them like wool. Shadowy rivers of mist, twice as thick as those from before, pushed through the stones in the floors and walls.

"Mists." Mazarine leaned against the bars, blinking heavily. "They create illusions to slow us, trap us into staying. They're what have been keeping me weak in this cage."

The room filled quickly with smog.

Cecelia shook the sleepy mists from her brain and calculated how to escape. "Mother, can you stand? We need to get out of here."

Mazarine nodded. "I think so."

Cecelia helped her up. Dark storms battled outside, whipping sands and howling winds. Trystyng and Phantasmagoria were out there somewhere. The mists had made her forget them.

Not anymore.

"Hold your breath as long as you can," Cecelia said, coughing. Mazarine nodded with puffed cheeks while Cecelia listened at the door.

The halls were silent. Where could the parent things have gone? If she led her real mother into the hall and those things attacked them, who knew what could happen? Even if Cecelia could fight them off, she didn't think her mother was strong enough to defend herself.

Make a decision, Cecelia.

Slowly and carefully, she opened the door and peered into the hall. The mists fogging the bedroom blew through the doorway and slithered along the floor to the right. Cecelia saw no evil paper things. At once, her mind began to defog. Cecelia inhaled fresh air and whispered, "Let's go. The coast seems clear."

Mazarine heaved mighty breaths. Cecelia's torn ankle wavered, but didn't bend. As they stepped into the hall, the mists vanished.

To their surprise, on the floor at their feet were a series of makeshift arrows pointing up the corridor to their right. But that wasn't the most extraordinary part: the arrows had been arranged with daisies.

Mother and daughter shared a glance. Mazarine shrugged. Cecelia swore the daisies weren't there earlier, but they'd never led her wrong before.

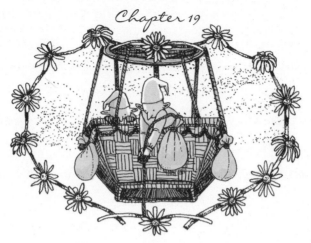

A Trail, a Lock, and an
Unusually Heroic Key

Lightness and darkness meandered the walls in shadows of orange and black. Cecelia and Mazarine followed the flowery arrows through the dim corridors this way and that, all the way to a bare stone wall.

"What now?" her mother whispered, wavering on noodling legs. Cecelia's paper limbs were still in good shape, yet her back had started to numb.

Cecelia inspected the passageway behind them, scanning the cracks between stones. She saw no mists or cruel paper ghouls. Why would the daisies and whoever left them lead Cecelia and her mother to a wall?

No, not a wall—a trapdoor.

Cecelia spotted the distinct outline in the stones. She and Mazarine pushed on the secret exit together, yet the door wouldn't open.

"Cecelia, do you see that?" Mazarine squinted at two symbols chiseled into the rock. The top one was small, deep, and oddly shaped, unlike the larger, more recognizable indentation underneath. "Do those two shapes look familiar to you?"

Cecelia cocked her head at the uppermost opening. It almost looked like a keyhole. Cecelia didn't have a proper key, but she did have a reasonable facsimile. She reached into her pocket and pulled out her mother's gift to her.

Mazarine's eyes sparked in a way Cecelia hadn't seen since her brother died. "You met the boy and his sheep!"

"I did." Cecelia had forgotten about their Joan of Arc until now. "Thank you for leaving it for me."

"It was the least I could do."

"I love you," Cecelia said.

"And I love you."

Head high, Cecelia raised the figurine and placed its sword tip in the hole, sure it would work. But the door remained fused shut.

"What about the shape below that one?" Mazarine asked. "What does it remind you of?"

Cecelia's eyes gleamed. "The head of a daisy."

Mazarine nodded. "Maybe if we use them together . . . ?"

"Yes." Cecelia grinned. "I'll hold the Joan key and you place the daisy key."

"On three," Mazarine said, picking up the nearest bloom.

Together they counted, "One, two, three."

When Mazarine placed the daisy into the opening, it hardened into a perfect key and fused with the stone. At the same time, Cecelia turned the Joan hard right.

The secret door opened. Heavy blocks slid soundlessly backward to reveal a hidden staircase going down. Winds, as cold as deep earth, pushed back their hair.

"Where do you think it leads?" Mazarine whispered into the depths of the black cavern.

"I don't know. But we can figure it out together." In the far reaches of her mind, Cecelia wondered why anyone would help them escape. She was quite sure the Land of Yesterday never let any of its prisoners go.

Maybe it was Phantasmagoria and Trystyng? A thrill of hope rose within her. Cecelia had been so worried about them since gaining back her unmisted faculties; they were never far from her thoughts. But why go to all this trouble? If the gnomes knew where she and her mother were, why not help them escape in person?

The secret door closed behind Cecelia and Mazarine,

enfolding them in darkness. Cecelia's lantern glowed softly through her parchment skin. Dim sconces, hung high on the turret, lit the way down the spiral staircase.

"Stay close to me," Cecelia whispered while scanning for mists. "Yesterday sneaks up when you least expect it." Studying her mother in the firelight, Cecelia frowned. Her midnight-blue paper tresses were peppered with the silver of a timber wolf's fur; all its spunk seemed gone. "I'll go first."

Crunching and crumbling echoes beat out of the dimness below. The stone staircase shook. The two stared at each other as dust rained from above.

"What was that?" Mazarine uttered.

"I don't know. Better keep going."

Tiny bits of debris littered the staircase from whatever had shaken the castle. So far, they had seen no mists or paper monstrosities. Still, Cecelia felt uneasy.

"Cecelia, your face . . ." Mazarine pointed to the left side of Cecelia's jaw.

Sure enough, when Cecelia ran her fingers from jawline to cheek, she found a length of paper. How much more of herself was affected, she wondered, if she hadn't even felt her face numb?

The castle rattled. Mazarine grabbed hold of her daughter, steadying her until the shaking passed. "Are you all right?"

Cecelia smiled. "I'm fine." A grating sound like stone against stone wound up through the stairwell. They exchanged nervous glances but stayed silent. The torches sputtered in an updraft of wind. "Come on. Maybe whoever's helping us is leading our way to the exit. Escaping Yesterday is our only hope." Cecelia took her mother's hand; when she clasped on, Mazarine's fingers went limp and slipped free.

"Cecelia?" Her mother paused on the steps to gape down at her paper abdomen. Her dress and the skin of her middle had thinned, enough to see a small tarnished cage and unlit lantern within her. The castle moaned and shifted around them. Mazarine slid to the ground. "What's happening to me?"

Cecelia sped to her mother's side. "It's okay—I have a cage, too, and my lantern wasn't lit at first either." Rocks crumbled from overhead. Cecelia's hair formed an umbrella above her mother to protect her. "I think everyone might have secret lanterns inside them. Lanterns that, when we're especially sad or scared, might go dark and need help lighting again. Sometimes it's the care of our family and friends that brings back our spark; other times, it's the care we give to ourselves. Either way, once we're relit, I think we can help reignite someone else." Cecelia took her mother's hand. "If we work together, I know we can make it."

Mazarine smiled bravely up at her like she used to, with a special beautifulness Cecelia vowed to protect, and then closed her eyes.

"Right." Cecelia scooped her mother up effortlessly—she weighed no more than a bouquet of daisies—and hurried down the rest of the stairs.

At the bottom, Cecelia found another door, this one of iron and wood. The torch above this exit illuminated a crushed, heart-shaped lock that someone—or -thing—had smashed open before their arrival.

Strange. Cecelia wondered if the gnomes were strong enough to break an iron lock. The disturbing paper dolls wouldn't help them escape, yet someone seemed to be.

Cecelia set Mazarine on the landing before the door. "I'm going to get us out of here. You wait and see."

The ground buckled. They sank into the collapsing stone. "Cecelia . . ."

The walls disintegrated. Bits of rubble fell like hail.

"Don't worry," Cecelia replied. "I can do this."

"Cecelia, the mists . . ."

Monstrous streams of black fog rolled down the staircase toward them, larger and uglier than ever. The torches on the walls extinguished at once.

Inside the slithering darkness, Cecelia focused on her

brother—that he had once lived—and that her father and mother needed her now more than ever. Cecelia whipped around, faced the mists, and roared, "We are stronger than forgetting, fiercer than the Land of Yesterday. We are hope. And hope thrives in the hopeless dark!"

Cecelia's lantern flared. A beam of light blasted into the mists. The black vapors shrieked and writhed and shrank back from her shine.

Mazarine cried out, "Cecelia, something's wrong. . . ."

Cecelia kicked open the door as the desert began to crumble like an earthquake at the end of the world.

An Unlikely Ally

The door flew open with a crack and a bang. Riotous winds ripped it free of its hinges and sucked it into oblivion. The mists on the stairway scattered into a million black smithereens and vanished with an angry shriek.

"Mother!" Cecelia called into the tempest.

Mazarine sat hunched over on the floor, eyes closed. Sand, blown in with the wind, coated her mother in a glitter of onyx dust. When Cecelia knelt before her, she noticed her mother's boots had papered. And that paper, like the rest of her mother's paper skin, didn't seem as strong as Cecelia's. Choking on desert, wind, and death, Cecelia knelt at her side. "Are you okay—can you walk?"

Her mother didn't answer. But just when Cecelia feared the worst, she witnessed a miracle. Mazarine Ignoscentia Dahl forced her eyes open, and stood.

"Oh souls," Cecelia exclaimed. "You're okay!"

Mazarine didn't look well. One of her hands was severely crumpled, her legs wibbled and wobbled unsteadily, yet she stepped into the door frame, regardless. Dress flapping like a paper flag, blue-and-silver hair whipping sharply sideways, she replied, "I'll be fine, thanks to you. A bit weak, but I think I can make it." Then, like magic, her mother's lantern sparked to life. The flame was small, but there.

"Wonderful." Cecelia's grin lit up her whole face. "Take my hand, let's—"

A terrible rumble, low and slow, issued from under their feet.

Rip.

Shred.

Shimmy.

Poised to walk through the door frame, they shared a *what was that?* glance.

CRACK.

The floor vibrated and lurched. Their cages rattled, lanterns trembled, and teeth chattered. The stairwell broke away from its foundation. The castle was shattering around them, and soon it would fall. "Take my hand," Cecelia shouted to her mother. "Hold tight and don't let go, even if my hand breaks!"

Mazarine nodded, squinting into the black storm. And then, with one last groan of rock tearing from earth, the hidden stairwell divided from Never More and Once Again. The turret of stairs and stone lifted with a groan and a whoosh.

"We're heading up," Cecelia hollered, hair flying. "Hang on!"

The stairwell pitched and swayed. Cecelia held her mother closer and peered into the thrashing desert below. Higher now, Cecelia saw everything—the castle, the wastes of Yesterday getting farther away, and the Haunted Galaxy of cobwebs and dust. The only thing left to wonder was, who was helping them escape?

The familiar hissing of a rocket blasting off roared overhead.

"What's that sound?" asked Mazarine.

Cecelia puckered her brow.

Could it be?

Pushing her face into the gale, Cecelia spied two ropes hooked to the turret currently hurtling toward space, and one extra-large black-and-white-striped hot-air balloon carrying them. "Trystyng and Phantasmagoria!" Cecelia cried. "It *is* them!"

Phantasmagoria and Trystyng, back to their nondog selves, clapped and cheered from the odd new Dröm Ballong. And beside them stood another someone as stalwart as the gnomes.

"Caterwaul! You came, too." The Caterwaul heaved the ropes attached to the turret until it could heave no more. Extending one giant arm, first to Mazarine, and then to Cecelia, the Caterwaul hauled them into a black wicker basket, twice the size of the last. The Cat Guardian set them down, and welcomed them each with a bow.

Cecelia ran at its furry girth and hugged it tight. "I've missed you." Then she moved on to the gnomes, who seemed to have given up their feud with the great cat. "And my dear friends, Phantasmagoria and Trystyng, I was so worried about you both." Cecelia embraced them at once. "Sorry I left you in the desert when I entered the castle. I didn't realize you'd gone. Still, you came back. Thank you." They shook their heads and waved her apologies away.

The Caterwaul cut the ropes to the staircase with one slice of its razor-sharp claws. The balloon lifted, wobbled, and swayed. And thanks to the stones piled high on one side of the basket to compensate for the Caterwaul's weight, it didn't upturn. Together, the motley crew watched the turret plunge through the black depths below. It crashed into a mountain of sand. Another lost, curious thing in Yesterday's desert.

Once the Dröm Ballong had steadied, Cecelia rejoined her mother and led her toward the gnomes. "Trystyng, Phantasmagoria, I'd like to introduce my mother, Mazarine Dahl." Cecelia glowed with pride. When Mazarine stepped forward on wobbly legs, Cecelia hurried to help her.

"Hello, brave masters." Mazarine nodded queenly to each gnome. "It is my absolute pleasure to finally meet you." After Phantasmagoria and Trystyng gave her an *aww, shucks* look, they removed their hats, bowed like gentlemen, and kissed the backs of her hands. Mazarine giggled and kissed their cheeks in return.

The gnomes blushed so furiously, Cecelia thought their ears might whistle and steam.

Next, Mazarine turned her attention to the Caterwaul and gave a chivalrous bow. "And I am honored to see you again, Caterwaul, especially under these pleasanter circumstances." Mazarine smoothed its great whiskers and planted a smooch on its cheek, too.

The tips of the Caterwaul's fur turned tomato red. *"Heeell-lloooo, Maaazzarriiiinnne,"* the Caterwaul purred, and offered the sweetest grin. *"The hoooonooooor iiis miiiiinnne."*

The Dröm Ballong bounced and bumped in the high

winds, and nearly knocked her mother off her feet. Once again, Cecelia—and her hair—reached out to help her.

"Where did you get this balloon, anyway?" Cecelia asked. "It's so much bigger than those before."

Trystyng and Phantasmagoria, busy checking this gauge and that lever, paused to point at the Caterwaul. The fur at the Caterwaul's cheeks blushed even darker than moments before. *"Maaade it forrr yoooooooou,"* the Caterwaul replied.

"You"—she paused—"made this, for *us*?"

Clasping its paws behind its back, the Caterwaul nodded and shuffled its feet. Stray daisy petals clung to the Caterwaul's furry coat. Mazarine plucked a few free, her lantern shining a little brighter.

Cecelia's hair blew forward and stroked the Caterwaul's fur. "You broke the Law of Yesterday and helped us, didn't you, Caterwaul? You braved the mists and left us a trail to the exit."

Trystyng and Phantasmagoria pointed at the Caterwaul, nodding so fast their hats tilted and spun.

Cecelia lunged at the giant bewhiskered beast and mumbled, "Thank you," into its soft coat. "And you two," Cecelia laughed. "You literally ripped the castle to bits to rescue us." Trystyng and Phantasmagoria shrugged nonchalantly and glanced at their feet. Cecelia hugged them once more.

Mazarine pulled the Caterwaul aside. "You are quite the hero, aren't you?" she commented with a sly glance. The Caterwaul growled pleasantly. "Why did you risk your position as Guardian to the Land of Yesterday to help us?"

The Caterwaul raised its silvery eyes onto Cecelia, fur blowing in the wind. *"Nobodyyyy everrr hugged the Caterwauuuul befoooore Ceceliaaaa hugged the Caterwauuuul. Nobodyyyy everrr showwwed Caterwauuuul suuuch lovvvve."* It turned back to Mazarine. *"Herrr giffft tooo meeee waaas the greaaaatest gifffft of aaaaall."*

Mazarine stroked her daughter's hair, like she had when Cecelia was small. Grateful, it nuzzled her back.

A sharp gust of wind shoved Cecelia and Mazarine sideways. Cecelia's broken ankle buckled; the bindings holding it together snapped. The Caterwaul caught them both before they sailed into space. After setting Mazarine down, the great cat lifted Cecelia, cradled her ankle in its paw, and grinned. *"III wiiill fiiiix yooou."*

It produced the pen she'd given it and shook a single sorrowful tear onto her fractured leg. Immediately, daisies sprouted from her skin. Their vines twisted upward, stitching together her broken halves; the vine then cut itself free, and wove into the new Dröm Ballong's basket, coating it in white-and-yellow blooms.

"You did it—you fixed me." She tested her new ankle,

twisting it this way and that. "It's wonderful, thank you."

"*Thank yooou,*" the Caterwaul roared. "*For fixiiing Cater-wauuuul's heaaarrrt.*"

"Oh." She blushed. "I didn't do anything, Caterwaul. You fixed your heart on your own. And," she whispered into its ear so only the cat could hear, "now that we're in reasonable shape, let's find my father. Then we can fix him, too, and be a family again." Cecelia frowned at her mother's frail skin as the Caterwaul set her down.

Before it's too late.

The Dröm Ballong skirted the black desert of Yesterday like a planet moving around a sun, heading to the other side. It soared through haunted space in search of Widdendream and her father, yet came up empty. Then suddenly, Cecelia spotted the most beautiful cranberry-orange sunrise peeking up in the distance. The closer they drew to the colorful dawn, the faster Cecelia's lantern flickered.

The last few times her lantern had pulsed that way, her father had been nearby. Her excitement mounted as the Dröm Ballong rounded Yesterday's other side.

Directly below them was an ocean dotted with daisies, waters of purple and gold, and a man in a yellow slicker rowing a small white rowboat. The same bearded man she'd spoken with when she'd fallen through Widdendream's floor back in Hungrig, the same one Lady and Lord Arnot claimed to have met.

"Aubergine told me once," Mazarine said to Cecelia, staring down at the same sea, "that the Land of Yesterday has two sides. One is dark as death and means to trap you, but the other is bright as hope and wants to free you." Mazarine cast a confident yet tired glance below. "That must be the other side of Yesterday."

"Yes," Cecelia answered softly. "The Sea of Tears."

Just then, like spinning paper tops, two photographs of Mazarine sailed by. Cecelia and her mother reached out and grabbed one each.

Together they uttered, "Widdendream."

In a lightning bolt of revelation, Cecelia knew where Widdendream was. She remembered the photographs of her mother strewn about Widdendream's attic. She remembered how on the nightmare planet, when Widdendream shouted at her in a gust of angry wind, photographs of Mazarine blew out. And how, when Widdendream blasted off the Planet of Nightmares, its burners sputtered and its body struggled to rise.

Widdendream had crashed into the Sea of Tears and left a trail of evidence behind.

Cecelia glanced at her frail mother and knew exactly

what she'd have to risk to rescue her father. But first, she'd have to come clean with her mother. Cecelia put on a brave face and told her everything. How Widdendream threatened her. How it hid her father away, hurt him, and ran. How it loathed Cecelia yet loved her mother and would do anything to have its best friend back. How it had become dark, evil, cold.

Mazarine digested Cecelia's every word—sadly, then angrily; and finally, she held her head high with new determination and an even stronger lantern flame. "It seems Widdendream has left us no choice."

"Follow the daisies," Cecelia said.

"Follow the daisies, indeed."

The battle wasn't over yet.

A Bittersweet Not-Goodbye

On the flip side of Yesterday, winds raged over Captain Shim's Sea of Tears. The balloon jostled in feuding gales. Daisies and leaves ripped from the Dröm Ballong's vines and circled them wildly. Mazarine clung to the Caterwaul's fur; it shielded her from the winds. Cecelia stood alone in the center of the hurricane and faced the gnomes.

"Trystyng! Phantasmagoria!" Cecelia shouted over the squall. "We need to see the Captain, right away."

Trystyng gave her a firm salute, and then did something she didn't expect. He opened his mouth to speak.

"Oh no!" Cecelia grasped the fraying vines. Her hair twined the ropes. She squeezed her eyes tight, bracing herself

190

for the gust about to blast from his mouth.

But the following softhearted words issued from the gruff gnome instead: "Your command is our duty, Miss Dahl."

Cecelia unclenched.

She understood him.

His words did not blow her away.

"Anything for you, Miss Cecelia," Phantasmagoria added with a bow. "Anything, always."

Before she had a chance to comment on the gnomes' lack of blustery language, Trystyng reeled about to face Phantasmagoria and the Caterwaul, all cordial niceties gone. "Well, what are you two lazy lots waiting for, Phantasmagoria and Caterwaul, do-nothing day? We've got a father to find, so let's get back to work!"

"Wait!" Cecelia grabbed Phantasmagoria and Trystyng, and laughed. "I understand you. How is that possible?"

Cecelia's hair clapped excitedly.

"You survived Yesterday, of course," Phantasmagoria answered with a cheerful grin.

Trystyng added grumpily, "Only those who escape Yesterday understand the language of Now." He shook his head, rolled his eyes, and said with a sigh, "Obviously." He peeked at Cecelia then and gave her the warmest smile of all.

"Really?" Cecelia beamed. "How wonderful!" She pulled

her friends to her and hugged them one more time, never wanting to let go.

The sun, the shade of fresh orange juice, hung halfway in and out of the sea.

Mazarine left the Caterwaul's side, pulled her daughter close, and kissed the top of her head. Their faces gleamed inside the strange citrusy light. "I wouldn't be here without your help. Thank you for coming for me, Cecelia."

Cecelia smiled up at her mother. "I will always come back for you."

The Dröm Ballong began its descent.

"Where will we land?" Cecelia noticed no islands or rocks.

"Don't worry," Trystyng bellowed. "We'll get you to the Captain safely."

"Hang on!" Phantasmagoria shouted. "We're coming in hot!"

The Dröm Ballong shuddered and shook and dropped. Freefalling toward the rowboat in the center of the sea, it slammed on the brakes midair, a car's length above the boat. The crew, shaken and definitely stirred, clambered to their feet. Cecelia helped her mother to rise.

"You know," Cecelia said, picking daisy petals and leaves from her hair, "in the future, I'd appreciate a bit more warning before . . ."

Trystyng and the Caterwaul avoided her eyes. Their faces lowered, mournful, sad. Phantasmagoria plucked one last daisy from Cecelia's tresses. His smile, heartbreaking and fateful, had the feeling of goodbye.

"Oh," Cecelia replied sadly, "I see. This is as far as you go, isn't it?"

Trystyng took Cecelia's hand and kissed the back like a proper gentleman. Her hair wiped tears from his unusually nongrumpy eyes, which made him cry even more. "Last stop, miss," he choked with a sob and a sniff. "This is the end of the . . . of the . . ."

Unable to finish his speech, Phantasmagoria lifted his chin and took the lead. "This is the end of the line for us, Miss Cecelia and Miss Mazarine." He bowed, smiling kindly, new steel in his eyes. "It has been our honor to serve you both. Perhaps, someday, you'll join us again for another adventure." He slipped his hat from his knobby head and bowed low to Mazarine; with a gracious grin, she bowed back. He winked at Cecelia and pulled her into the greatest, gnomeiest hug of her life.

Cecelia's lantern grew even brighter.

Trystyng and Phantasmagoria stepped aside and let the Caterwaul through. The Guardian of Yesterday dropped to one knee and held its big, fuzzy arms out to Cecelia.

"Oh, Caterwaul. You're not leaving, too, are you?" Even

as Cecelia said the words, she knew the answer. She buried her face in its warmth, trying to imprint this moment into her forever memory.

The Caterwaul purred, *"Nooot goodbyyye. Aaall you haaave to dooo is rememberrr meeee, and I willll beeee with yooou agaaaaaain."*

Her lantern brightened even more.

Cecelia watched the Caterwaul bid her mother farewell. Hurt and love and loss and friendship and laughter and thankfulness thrummed as one new emotion inside her being. She didn't want to leave the gnomes or the Caterwaul, having grown so fond of her new friends, whom she loved like family—farts, claws, and all. But then Cecelia realized something: she loved them enough to let them go.

Below them, waves slapped the side of the Captain's rowboat. A serene pleasantness emerged from each deep wrinkle of the Captain's weathered face. Purple lightning flashed in his beard as he peered up at them.

"I guess this is it, then," Cecelia said. "Trystyng, Phantasmagoria, Caterwaul, I hope one day we meet again."

Since the balloon could lower no more, Cecelia and her mother clasped hands and leaped into Captain Shim's boat together. By the time they settled on the boat's bench, the balloon had begun drifting away.

The gnomes held their tiny hats at their chests and waved

at them with their free hands; they appeared to be sniffing back tears. Cecelia's hair reached toward the balloon. The Caterwaul held a paw up in a still wave.

Farewell, Cecelia thought, *not goodbye.*

Mazarine stroked her daughter's anxious hair until it calmed. "Letting go is just another way to love, isn't it? I see that now." Four crystalline tears plinked from her eyes to the floor. "We carry those we love in our hearts always, no matter where or how far we go."

Cecelia took a deep breath and hugged her mother gently. "Yes," Cecelia replied, thinking of her brother. "I believe you're right."

Captain Shim, sitting opposite them, had observed quietly until now. He tipped his hat to Mazarine and Cecelia. "Nice to see you again, Daughter of Paper and Tears, and you, too, Mother of the same."

Mazarine slumped against Cecelia, barely able to sit upright. Lantern light shone through the cracks in her mother's skin. Parchment crawled up and over her knees. Mazarine grew frailer each time Cecelia looked at her, which prompted her to check her own skin. The left side of Cecelia's face had fully papered, and the right was well on its way. Her lower and middle back, too.

They needed to make this quick.

"I'll get right to the point, Captain. We've come to rescue my father from the mad house that kidnapped him. I suspect it crashed into your sea."

One of Mazarine's hands, crumpled and torn in the castle, slipped into the shimmering waters. The daisies riding the waves went to work to fix her. Her hand surfaced wearing a long glove of white blooms that held her together, good as new.

"I always knew you'd figure out the right place and time for a rescue"—Captain Shim gestured toward her lantern and winked—"bright girl that you are. Your house passed over my sea trying to keep up with you, sure. However, its spirit wasn't strong enough to sustain its burners. It crashed into my waters and sank. You followed the clues successfully, with the help of family and friends." Cecelia flushed. When she looked for the balloon next, it was gone. Shim continued, "I know leaving them was hard. But knowing when to let go is one of the most important lessons we can learn in life, and you managed it with grace."

"Thank you, Sea Captain." Cecelia nodded to him and then turned to face her mother. "Before we go, in case anything should happen to either of us, I need to tell you something else. Something that might hurt you."

"You can tell me anything," Mazarine said.

Cecelia took a quick breath. "Celadon's spirit came to me." Instant tears sprang to her mother's eyes; Cecelia wiped them away. "But leaving Yesterday cost him dearly. The last time I saw him was on the Planet of Nightmares. He led me to a secret passageway into Yesterday right before . . ." Not knowing how to continue, Cecelia simply opened the doors of herself and unlocked her cage. And there, leaning against her lantern—now untarnished, shining, and clean—was her paper brother, no bigger than Cecelia's hand.

"Oh." Mazarine covered her mouth. "Is that . . . Is it really . . . ?"

"It's him." Cecelia wrung her hands. "I didn't want to lose him again. But it happened anyway."

"I know, Cecelia," her mother said, pulling her close.

"Would you like to carry him? I bet he'd like it if you sang some of your old songs. You know how he always loved that."

Mazarine nodded and sputtered a wistful laugh. "Oh, yes. I'd like that very much." Cecelia passed her mother what remained of her lost child. Carefully, with the hand gloved in daisies, Mazarine opened the center of herself right above her navel, in a neat door shape. She unlocked her rusted cage, and set Celadon at the base of her own lantern, just south of her heart. In a great burst, Mazarine's lantern brightened and spilled over with pure white light. "There." Mazarine sniffed. "My boy is safe and sound. Now we go rescue your father."

Their paper doors closed. The time had come to make their move.

With that thought, hundreds of daisies gathered alongside the boat and began weaving a stairway to the bottom of the sea. The last time Cecelia had submerged in these waters, she ended up falling through space.

"My daisies are ready when you are," Captain Shim said with a lighthearted grin.

The boat rocked and creaked. Mazarine was the first to stand. "Come on, Cecelia," she said, chin high, one paper boot on the boat's rim. "If Joan of Arc, not much older than you are now, could lead a holy rebellion, then surely we can submerge in an ocean of tears and down a stairway of daisies. Are you with me?"

With confidence, Cecelia answered, "I am." She perched alongside her mother and bowed to Captain Shim. "Thank you, Captain, for everything."

"Don't mention it." He tipped his hat and winked. "Sometimes all you can do is trust you'll find your way home."

Chapter 22

A STAIRWAY TO THE BOTTOM OF THE SEA

Hands clasped, Cecelia and her mother descended into the unknown. Their teeth chattered. Their hair flowed out behind them—Cecelia's in streamers of blue, Mazarine's in moonlit silver. The Sea of Tears moved in and out of their lungs as naturally as air as they followed the daisy staircase down.

The water surrounding them echoed with haunted cries. Mourning mothers, hungry babies, children whose little brothers had died. Songs of the sorrowful pressed in as tight and cold as the ghostly weeds reaching up to grab them. Yet the thrill of finding Aubergine fluttered like metal wings inside their cages. And that was enough to keep them moving fearlessly forward.

Cecelia kept glancing back at her mother to make sure she hadn't fallen apart. The only visible fragments of Mazarine that remained unpapered were on her lower neck and collarbone. Much of Cecelia's neck had turned, as had more of her right cheek, though most of her upper back was still flesh, and, she guessed, so was her still-beating heart. Bits of shredded parchment flaked from their softening limbs as they moved through the water. If they didn't save Father soon, the sea might devour them.

Icy water slipped past, chilling as a grave. No fish lived in this sea; nothing seemed alive except for them. Bubbles swirled around their bodies, echoing as they popped. Daisy petals floated by like delicate jewels, along with a single photo, this time of the Dahls, Widdendream and all. Her mother fell behind only once. After Mazarine became tangled in willowy vines, Cecelia rushed back and worked the knots with softening fingers until her mother slipped free. Exhausted and broken, but more determined than ever, they finally reached the bottom of the sea.

The water down below was darker and as cold as snow. Feet wobbling, they glanced about. Everything was murky and dim. Mazarine and Cecelia stepped wearily off the daisy steps and onto the rippled underwater sands.

Behind them, the daisies untwisted from the staircase

they'd built of themselves and then, all at once, undulated through the shimmering water toward Cecelia and Mazarine. First the blooms sniffed their wounds and the rips in their perforated paper skin like curious dogs. Then they sprang. Twining their broken bodies, binding each bend and rip until *zip-zap-bang*, Cecelia and her mother were dressed in the finest daisy armor anyone in any world had ever seen.

Mazarine and Cecelia tested their arms, fingers, legs, and toes, stretching, flexing, grinning from ear to ear. They found their armor sound and wonderful; their lantern light shone through the cracks. Together, they bowed to the daisies. And together, the daisies bowed back. Those that remained shot toward the surface, back to Captain Shim. Cecelia and her mother waved another not-quite goodbye.

Something flashed in the water ahead.

Twin spotlights, angled like furious eyes, turned toward them in the distance. Cecelia would know their shape anywhere. The last time Cecelia had seen these particular lights, their owner had been unable to turn them on. Due to Mazarine leaving home, the owner of these lights was forced to use candles instead. But now the window-eyes blazed with electricity, casting back and forth as if surprised by the sudden outpouring of light. A photograph of Mazarine playing tea party with a cheerful Widdendream bobbed past Cecelia's nose. A noxious odor spread through the sea from the direction of the glow; the same moldy green stink that had plagued their house since that first evil Tuesday. They'd done it. Together, they'd found Widdendream.

The lantern flickered in Cecelia's cage: her father was still inside.

Black water moved past Widdendream, smudging its already foreboding appearance. The attic swiveled as it scanned the base of the sea. Cecelia wasn't sure if it could see them or not.

Mazarine gave her a grave look. "Stay close to me." Despite their being underwater, their voices rang clear, if not a little warbly.

"No," Cecelia replied. "It wants you in return for releasing Father. Who knows if, once Widdendream has you, it'll even let him go? And who knows what it'll do to you if you go inside? I should face Widdendream alone."

"Absolutely not," Mazarine answered in a motherly voice of authority. "Warm and luminous things often infuriate cold and shadowy things. Which is why, if we're going to sneak inside and rescue your father, we'll have to look out for each other. I won't let you do this alone. We must stick together."

Cecelia sighed. "Maybe you're right."

"I know I am." Mazarine winked.

Cecelia's hair shook with amusement. "Even still, take this for luck, okay?" Cecelia dug past the daisies and reached inside her pocket, then placed Joan of Arc in her mother's hand.

Mazarine lit with pride and clutched it tight. "For luck."

The sound of furniture breaking echoed from Widdendream's attic. Shadows crossed its windows as Aubergine let out a sharp cry.

Big-eyed with worry, Cecelia whispered, "Father."

"I know," Mazarine replied. "Let's go."

The light within Widdendream brightened the closer Mazarine drew. The outside remained dark as night. Concealed in the watery shadows, Cecelia and Mazarine swam to the back of the house. Every crack and hole in Widdendream's outer shell had been chinked with seaweed and sludge, keeping the inside airtight and water-free. Still, Widdendream had neglected to lock the cellar doors. "When you enter," Cecelia told her, "Widdendream might know."

Mazarine gave a curt nod. Then, as quietly as possible, she opened the cellar doors. Seawater rushed down the stone steps. Mazarine submerged into the basement with the flood, and raised their Joan of Arc high. "Onward," she said with a grin, and vanished into the dark.

Cecelia followed in a dim circle of shine and closed the doors behind her.

The bare bulb in the cellar flashed on. The seawater that had rushed in with them came up to their knees, and lit with a brackish green glow. Tiny rivulets of water ran down the walls. Fruits and vegetables that Cecelia and her mother had canned together still sat on the shelves, same as they always had. Except now, the floating jars looked sinister. Like eyeballs and brains and dead things, setting their focus on her.

A steady *bang-bang-bang* echoed from the attic—undoubtedly from her father. In the background, Widdendream howled a string of distracted and mournful cries: "It's their fault she left, not mine, never mine—how could they do this to me?"

Mazarine climbed the stairs that led to the kitchen. She paused at the door, and faced Cecelia. Water dripped from her hair and armor of daisies with soft little *plink*s. Mazarine mouthed, *Attic,* and pointed at the door, and then, *Stay quiet. Don't stop running for anything.*

Cecelia nodded and pushed her worries from mind: how best to protect her mother while saving her father from further harm, how not to lose the last of her flesh before that happened.

Mazarine opened the door to the kitchen. A thin layer of water streamed out from the kitchen and spilled down the steps. Seaweed and bottom-of-the-sea muck patched the fissures inside the house, too. Other than a few leaks, Widdendream's interior didn't seem too badly flooded.

A scream ripped through the house from Aubergine—painful, tortured, and deafening. Without thinking, Mazarine cried out, "Aubergine!" She quickly covered her mouth, but the damage was done.

The attic noise ground to a halt. Widdendream had heard her cry.

A low vibration hit the groundwater. Jars of flour and sugar, coffee, and herbal teas trembled on the countertops. The refrigerator door banged open and closed as the rumble increased. Shadows slithered across the waterlogged floors and clawed up and down the walls. The structure of the house shrank and expanded. Then, for an infinity of seconds, everything stilled.

Until slowly, Widdendream's voice reverberated through time and space and the truth of all things. "At last," Widdendream said with a sigh. "You've come back to me. . . ."

Chapter 23

THE MYSTERIOUS TORMENT
SURROUNDING AUBERGINE

The lights in the kitchen flashed on, illuminating everything.

"Mazarine." Widdendream's voice shivered through the drowned house like thunder. "Mazarine, please, speak to me."

Crouched in ankle-deep water behind the island in the center of the kitchen, Cecelia seized her mother's hand. She could see by her anxious and angry expression, she wanted to give Widdendream a piece of her mind. Cecelia shook her head at her mother, silently urging her to stay quiet.

With a sigh, Mazarine nodded and let her daughter take the lead.

"Mazarine, I know you're here . . . my *friend*, please . . . ," Widdendream pleaded, "at least let me know you're all right."

Widdendream seemed both relieved and concerned about her mother's well-being. It sounded so much like its old self Cecelia didn't know how to feel. If her home retained enough heart to love, maybe there was still hope. Maybe, one day, Widdendream could overcome the darkness that had taken over its gentle soul.

Follow me, Cecelia mouthed to her mother. When she unfroze from her place in the kitchen and sprang, Mazarine followed.

Together, they sprinted as fast as their daisy armor could carry them. They hurried past the breakfast nook, where they used to eat pancakes. They pushed beyond the island and stools, where Cecelia and Celadon used to make funny faces at each other, laughing until they cried. Moving through the family dining room, they passed the table and Celadon's empty chair, and all the ghosts of their past.

"Mazarine, don't shut me out. I'm not myself without you. You're the only one I"—Widdendream's voice cracked—"you're the only one I have left!"

Cecelia glanced back at her mother. Mazarine shook her head and mouthed, *Don't listen. Find your father.* She had to get her mother out of the house before Widdendream captured her, too.

Mother and daughter waded quickly up the hallway. The walls were damp. Water leached through Widdendream's patched holes and cracks, and soon began to rise. Scraps of paper on the water's surface clung to their ankles like cold little hands. Yet the closer they got to the attic, the stronger their lantern lights grew.

They were almost to the stairs when a rogue wave rolled out of the library and knocked Mazarine down. By the time Cecelia realized what had happened, Widdendream had shoved a bookcase between them.

"Please, Mazarine," Widdendream moaned in haunted tones. "Why do you ignore me? Why do you run from me? *I don't understand!*"

Cecelia kicked and shoved at the bookcase, but it was too heavy for her weak paper arms, even with her armor of daisies, to move.

From behind the bookcase, her mother shouted, "You aren't the home I remember, Widdendream. You've hurt the family you were supposed to protect. And you've hurt me."

"That's not true. We—we helped each other. I could never hurt you—you're the only one who's ever understood me." Widdendream trembled with a sadness so complete she thought it might give up all together. "I'm sorry if I hurt you. I never meant to hurt anyone—unlike your daughter and that liar Aubergine!" The emotion in its voice was so real and raw. Cecelia almost felt sorry for it.

Almost.

"My husband may be a lot of things, Widdendream, but he is no liar."

Widdendream roared.

Upstairs, Aubergine pounded the walls, shouting, "Mazarine, Cecelia, I know why it's doing this, it—"

BAM-BAM-*THWACK*.

Aubergine said no more.

Any sympathy Cecelia felt for Widdendream withered. Narrowing her eyes, Cecelia, the daisies, and her hair latched onto the case of books and slid it sideways, just enough for Cecelia to squeeze through.

"Come on," Cecelia whispered to her mother. "Let's go."

Side by side, they entered the foyer and started up the stairs. Lights flashed on as they went. Mazarine lost a chunk of hair along the way and Cecelia's knees kept giving out. Widdendream shook the staircase and surrounding water, trying to knock them down the steps. Almost to the second floor, Cecelia and Mazarine passed the once-broken knob at the top of the banister. They clasped hands, shared a brave smile, and kept going.

Nearing the attic stairs, the temperature dropped. The paintings, wallpaper, floors, their skin, and even the daisies binding them whitened with a kiss of frost. The water grew exceedingly cold. Despite the chill, their ever-brightening lanterns kept them warm.

"Cecelia Dahl!" The floors shuddered with Widdendream's voice. Yet neither Cecelia nor Mazarine paused. They continued upward and onward toward Aubergine. "Since your mother has sided with the enemy, our deal is off. You know what happens next."

Cecelia turned to her mother in panic. "It's going to hurt Father—permanently."

Mazarine's steps quickened. "We're not going to let it."

While they climbed the tiny staircase to the attic, Aubergine called out from inside. "Cecelia, Mazarine!" His voice sounded strained. "Is that you?"

Mazarine flung herself at the door, unconcerned with the barbed black vines snaking the wood. "Aubergine! You don't know how good it is to hear your voice."

"Oh souls, I have missed you both terribly." His delight turned serious fast. "But we don't have much time. . . . You won't like what I've become. You should run while you have the chance."

Cecelia and Mazarine shared a determined yet weary glance. "What are you talking about?" Mazarine asked. Each word squeezed with worry. "What has Widdendream done to you?"

A massive *SMASH* interrupted his answer, followed by a

muffled cry. They stood before the locked entrance, hearts thundering, hair undulating in slow arcs. Cecelia, trying not to think about her forehead going numb or that her back felt more and more paperish, grasped the doorknob and set her jaw.

"Are you ready?" Mazarine asked, wavering slightly on her feet. Her mother's cage had broken through her skin. Her neck had fully papered, along with much of her collarbone. The only things holding her up were the daisies. Cecelia didn't know exactly how much flesh her mother had left, but she knew it couldn't be much.

"Ready," Cecelia answered, pushing her fear away.

"Enter and die, Dahl family—CRUMBLE TO DUST LIKE MY HEART!" The attic shook as hard as a snow globe. Lightning cracked through the water; every light bulb in the house surged.

"Never!" Cecelia shouted. "Stand back if you can, Father. We're coming in."

Mother and daughter rammed the door so hard it blew off its hinges with a jagged *crack*. Cecelia and Mazarine tumbled into the attic and fell on top of each other. Still, with the help of their armor, they rose.

The bare bulb burst with light, as bright as a comet. Soggy cardboard boxes, old clothes, and shreds of parchment undulated through the thin layer of water covering the floor. Family photos, most of Mazarine, skimmed the surface. The heavier things—old lamps, dusty chairs, stacks of books—occupied the corners. Thorn-covered vines and black rot wound between everything yet did not move. Cecelia scanned the dim attic but found no sign of her father.

Out of the darkness, a voice floated softly toward them. "Hello, my loves."

Aubergine's words emerged from the back-corner shadows, slow and strange.

"Aubergine?" Mazarine dived toward the back wall, chasing his voice. Something stirred near the corner, like wind ruffling the pages of a book. "Where are you?"

"Sorry, Dahls," Widdendream interrupted, sounding closer than ever before. "Daddy has become a bit too"—its attic eyes turned up as if it was grinning—"*attached* to me to come out and play."

Heart beating behind her eyes like a bird trapped in her skull, Cecelia followed her mother toward the back of the room.

Mazarine screamed.

"Mother?" Lantern flickering wildly, Cecelia froze.

"Cecelia!" Mazarine cried through her fingers and faced the side wall. "Your father," she choked. "Oh, Widdendream, what have you done?"

Chapter 24

THE HIDEOUS TRUTH

A thatch of hair, a section of dark purple suit, and a select few fingers and toes poked out from the shredding wall.

"Oh souls," Cecelia gasped, legs weak. Not only had most of her father turned into paper, but Widdendream had sucked him into the wall and made him a part of it. "Widdendream, why did you do this? You said you'd let him go!"

Widdendream laughed under its breath. The water rippled and swayed with its reply. "You failed to keep your promises to me, so why should *I* keep mine to *you*?"

The daisies armoring Cecelia and Mazarine growled and lunged at the walls like a pack of rabid dogs.

"Cecelia." Aubergine's face scrunched tighter as the wall

pulled him in further. He struggled not to choke. "I'm sorry. I didn't want you to see me like this." Mazarine dropped to her knees before her husband. He eyed his wife like a last good-bye. "And look at you." Aubergine smiled lovingly. "Always so beautiful. Gods, I've missed you, Maz."

Cecelia and her mother each grasped what they could of his hands, and stared into his eyes—one of flesh, one of paper.

"And I have missed you." Mazarine kissed his cheek. Diamond-like tears bobbed around her and then floated away, caught in her dim lantern light.

Every muscle in Cecelia's body clenched. Biting back her own tears, she turned away from her father and addressed Widdendream. "Why are you hurting him? He's never done anything to you."

"That's a laugh. All your father's ever done is damage me, leave me to clean up his mess, and then try to abandon me, too. You don't know how it feels to spend every bit of energy, day in and day out, keeping those who depend on you safe, only to have them neglect you, mistreat you, and dismiss you!"

Seawater roiled around their feet, bubbling with rage.

Widdendream shifted its window eyes onto Mazarine. "When you were leaving, I was worried, scared. Your tears seeped into my floor as you paced. I wanted to help, but you wouldn't let me. Then you walked out the door without even saying goodbye."

The floors trembled and lights flashed. Cecelia moved closer to her mother and father and clasped their hands.

Widdendream glared at Aubergine. "Then *he* just let you go—sail off to this wasteland of tears and death from where no living things return! A real friend would have stopped you from leaving me. But you left anyway, and I've never felt more alone!"

Widdendream's thunderous howls ripped through the room as it dragged Aubergine deeper into the wall.

"Widdendream, stop!" Cecelia cried. "I'm the reason this all began. I was the one who neglected you the past few years. I was a terrible friend, and you didn't deserve that. I am truly sorry for hurting you, for not being there for you, for breaking my promise that fateful night. . . . I swore to check on you, glue the knob back on your broken banister if you were too ill for the job. But I fell asleep, and Celadon died." Cecelia's hair curled lovingly around her neck. "I'd do anything to take it all back. But I can't. I'm the one who deserves your wrath. So please, take me, but leave my parents alone."

The churning water stilled to slow waves. Widdendream

stopped absorbing Aubergine. Maybe it would let her father go after all?

Lantern shining through her armor, Mazarine pushed herself to her feet and addressed Widdendream. "I'm sorry, too, old friend, for leaving you the way I did." Mazarine stared straight into its attic-window eyes. "Sometimes, when we're grieving, the choices we make are selfish ones. It's a form of survival. We don't mean to hurt anyone, but occasionally, that's just what happens, isn't it? I beg, if our friendship ever meant anything to you, don't blame my husband and daughter for something I've done. The Widdendream I knew and loved wouldn't do that."

The temperature dropped lower. The walls themselves seemed to scream, "The Widdendream you knew is gone. Thanks to your daughter and what *she did* to our boy. It's *her* fault I became this monster!"

Aubergine strained to push his vanishing mouth forward. He focused on a hole in the baseboard at the bottom of the opposite wall, usually covered by piles of junk. Aubergine choked, seeming to sip words from the sea: "The truth is, you feel equally to blame for Celadon's death, don't you, Widdendream?"

The floor warped and swayed. A sudden blast of water and attic debris pushed Mazarine and Cecelia across the room.

217

"Stop now, Aubergine," Widdendream roared. "Or you will regret it."

As Cecelia and her mother fought their way back, Cecelia's mind reeled. Could guilt be making Widdendream act this way? Widdendream's rage had begun right after Celadon's death. And the attic that held its spirit had turned dark and poisonous, which was exactly the way Cecelia's guilt made her spirit feel. But why would Widdendream feel responsible when Cecelia had accepted the blame?

As her mother made it safely to her father's side, Cecelia remembered Celadon's nightmare: *Something pushes me and then I fall.*

Had something else happened the night her brother died that drove their kindhearted home to its cruel-hearted ways? Maybe if Cecelia could get Widdendream to open up about its guilt, she could help it expel the poison stuck in its spirit? Maybe then it would stop hurting her parents and this nightmare would end.

"Widdendream . . . ," Aubergine pleaded. The right side of his mouth disappeared behind the wall. "Be reasonable, just liste—"

"*ENOUGH!*" Widdendream drew the last of Aubergine's feet and arms through, until all that remained of him was his eggplant-colored lapels and the paper half of his face.

"Widdendream," Mazarine implored from Aubergine's side. "You must stop this, please, for me."

The curtains over the attic windows closed. Widdendream moaned with deep sorrow yet did not answer. Cecelia faced the black hole at the base of the far wall that her father had focused on earlier.

If she was going to save her family, the time to act was now.

"I know something else happened the night Celadon died, Widdendream." Cecelia strode confidently toward the ratlike hole. The water rolled and bubbled, splashing against her shins. Her entire face had papered, and much of her back felt paper-numb. Strands of hair broke from her scalp and drifted to the tattered ceiling; they tried to swim back to Cecelia but were lost in the current of tears. Nonetheless, Cecelia persisted. "Something that made you feel ashamed."

"No," Widdendream snarled. The sea grew denser, colder. A flair of nervousness rippled through the damp air. "You know *nothing*!"

"Widdendream?" Mazarine's lantern light had dimmed significantly. Her hair undulated in silver waves toward what remained of Aubergine. "What are they talking about?"

In a flurry of daisies and hair, Cecelia continued. "You had something to do with Celadon's death, didn't you?

219

Something that made you feel guilty enough to hide it, even from the one you considered your best friend." Widdendream cried out like a frightened animal. The waters stilled. Cecelia stopped before the hole in the baseboard, her back to her parents. "If you care for Mother as much you claim, you'll tell her the truth. After all, she forgave me. She might do the same for you."

"I don't deserve forgiveness," Widdendream replied. "You hurt me, Cecelia. I lost everything because of you, and now you'll lose the same."

"Cecelia . . ." Mazarine's panicked voice sliced through her thoughts, followed closely by a muffled cry. "Cecelia, oh souls—"

Widdendream almost sounded sorry when he said, "Say goodbye, paper girl."

Cecelia swung around just in time to witness the rest of her father vanishing into the wall and her mother, daisy armor and all, entering alongside him right after. "No!"

Mazarine, halfway absorbed, struggled to free herself to no avail. Cecelia pulled at her mother, but she wouldn't come free. Her paper skin chafed off in Cecelia's hands. The last of her mother's light drained away. "Widdendream," Cecelia cried. "Give them back this instant!"

"It's no use, Cecelia," Widdendream said softly, maybe

even sincerely. "I'm taking them from you, as you took your mother and brother from me. Maybe now you'll understand how it feels to be truly abandoned by those you love."

"Cecelia!" Mazarine's boots, hands, and her cage—with Celadon's paper ghost still inside—protruded from the wall. Wide-eyed and frantic, Mazarine whispered, "Never forget how much I love—" Her mother's voice cut off. The wall swallowed her hair and the daisies and her heartbreakingly familiar face in one gulp.

Cecelia's lantern suddenly brightened, illuminating the last of her mother—a single extended hand. Cecelia grasped her mother's hand for the last time. Mazarine's fingers opened like a budding daisy to reveal an object: the tiny likeness of Joan of Arc, which Cecelia had told her mother only moments ago to hold for luck. Cecelia curled her fingers around the idol. A breath later, her mother's fingers vanished.

"No!" Cecelia pounded and ripped at the wall where her parents went in. "No, no, no!" But the more she clawed and scraped, the faster her fingers crumpled and bent and turned to pulp under her daisy armor. No matter what Cecelia tried, she couldn't break through the wall. Cecelia dropped her hands to her sides. "Widdendream, where are they? What have you done with my parents?"

The house replied in an echoing boom, "I've made them a part of me."

All grew silent as the reality of the moment sank in:

1. Her father and mother were gone.

2. Cecelia was the last paper Dahl.

3. She could not let Widdendream take her.

Jaw clenched, lantern dim, and breath fast, Cecelia fought to control her anger. She was angry at Widdendream for not telling her what happened that night and turning evil. Angry at falling apart. Angry that her parents were gone and that Celadon had died. And now she was angry at her whole family, including herself, for not taking better care of the home they loved that had always been there for them.

Maybe that was the difference between her and Widdendream, Cecelia thought suddenly as she willed her breath to slow. No matter what she was going through, she always had someone at her side who believed in her, who helped her be strong and brave and kind when she didn't know how. Even when Cecelia made mistakes and it wasn't easy, she always had someone who loved her anyway. But in Widdendream's time of need, it had had no one, not even Mazarine.

Maybe Widdendream needed someone to show it the same loving care.

Maybe I could be that someone.

And maybe then Widdendream would give my mother and father back.

"Widdendream, come out from behind your walls. Let me see you face-to-face."

No answer.

Cecelia knelt before the opening at the baseboard, lamplight spilling all around her. "I know you're angry with me. I admit, what you did just now made me angry, too. But like it or not, we're family. And families, well, we make mistakes, don't we? We mess up and hopefully learn from it. If you come out and let me show you how sorry I am, maybe we could be friends who laugh and help each other, like we used to be, instead of enemies who hurt each other, like we are now." Cecelia heard a distant sniff. "If you do this one thing, I'll leave you alone. If that's what you want. I'll leave and never return."

Cecelia dug past the daisies twining her sweater pocket and dropped mini Joan inside. As she did, her fingers bumped against her miraculous pen of tears.

The Caterwaul must have returned it in secret.

A rusty echo creaked out from the small entrance before her. Cecelia peered inside. A hatch within the hole flipped open.

Cecelia leaned in closer.

A miniature Victorian cage, similar to the one inside Cecelia and her mother, perched deep in the shadows. Yet this cage had no lantern and had nearly corroded to dust. Another creak and the cage door opened.

A pair of glowing eyes blinked on in the hidden dark.

Chapter 25

WIDDENDREAM'S CONFESSION

A person-shaped being made of sour green mist emerged from the decaying cage in the hole of the baseboard. When the door of the small creature's enclosure slammed shut behind it, the cage crumbled to dust. Immediately, the attic fouled with an overpowering scent of rot. Cecelia tightened her fist around the pen in her pocket and held her breath as the spirit stepped out into the light.

A dark-green *W* marked its chest. The spirit, no bigger than Cecelia's hand, moved forward as if every breath it took ached. It shielded its eyes from the glow of her lantern like a creature too long in the dark and regarded her with a defiant glare. Yet, within its large black eyes, Cecelia saw a surplus of pain. She hurt for what it once was: a shining and beautiful soul, and a most kindred friend.

"You'll never make it out of here, you know," the decrepit spirit told Cecelia. "We are divergent, abnormal, broken. The Sea of Tears eats things like us alive." It gestured to the submerged floors. "See what it did to my handsome black vines? They're all but useless now, like me." When it glanced up at her, she thought she saw a faint flash of light in its dark eyes.

"You're Widdendream's spirit." This was not a question.

The tiny crooked thing groaned. "Before your family ruined me, perhaps. But now," it snapped, "I'm an ugly lost thing. I am sad, cold, and alone—*as I deserve to be.*"

Cecelia wanted to hate it for taking her family and causing them so much pain. Yet she couldn't help but feel sorry (and partly responsible) for its actions, as she knew how heavy a burden dark hearts could be.

Maybe, Cecelia thought, while staring into the dim light in its eyes stubbornly trying to ignite, if she could draw that light out, she could help them both.

"What I said about Celadon before you took my parents into your walls was true, wasn't it?" The small green spirit growled at her. Cecelia's hair swayed threateningly in a visual roar in reply. "You feel at least partly responsible for his death. But if Celadon's fall down the stairs was an accident, and fixing the banister was my responsibility, then why should you feel guilty at all?" Anguish twisted its face. Still kneeling before it, Cecelia leaned closer and softened her voice. "I know how much you loved Celadon, Widdendream, and doubt you'd hurt him on purpose, but if there's something I don't know about how he died, please tell me so we can move on."

Widdendream's spirit reeled as if slapped. "I would have never done anything to hurt any of you purposely—I loved the Dahl family without question or measure!" It turned its back and paced through the water up to its knees. "Not that it matters anymore. Don't you get it? There *is* no moving on from here. Without a family, I have no purpose. That's why I left my cage, which house spirits never do because once we leave, our cages crumble, and then . . . we die." The soul spun to face her. "And soon after, our houses die, too. It's over, Cecelia. So do me a favor, and leave me alone."

Cecelia reached out and grabbed its frigid hand. "Sorry, Widdendream, but you don't get to dismiss me that easily. I've lost a lot, too. Besides," she continued as the slippery soul pulled away, "if what you say is true, then what have you got to lose?"

The grim soul stared at her a long time before it relented

with a sigh. "Very well. If you're so interested in hearing about the devastating string of events that occurred that dreadful night, I'll tell you." Dual sparks blazed in its eyes. "Like all good tragedies, this story begins with love."

When a horrible truth drew near, fear tagged along, no matter how brave the one receiving that truth had grown.

Cecelia clutched her pen tighter, bracing for what was to come.

"Long ago, when my walls were sturdy and my paint fresh, I was truly a sight to behold. One of the first homes in Hungrig, I settled alone on the largest hill. The air was crisp and clean. Daisies sprang up at my feet. I had the mountains and lake for a view. It was wonderful. But inside, I was empty."

"You had no family." Cecelia glanced back at the wall into which her family had entered and never returned. Photographs of their happy faces drifted lazily upon the groundwater in currents of tears. She pushed back the steel lump of sadness rolling up her throat and turned around to face the small sad soul. "That must have been lonely."

Widdendream nodded, staring out the dark attic windows and into the sea. "It was—at first. But soon, new families came. Some I loved, some I liked, others I didn't understand at all. Yet every family that moved in treated me as if I were an object, a soulless structure without a heart, mind, or feelings—until your mother's family came along." It regarded Cecelia with a shy glance, its mist brighter than moments before. "Until Mazarine arrived, no one had even bothered to give me a name."

Cecelia smiled fondly. "I remember Mother telling me that story. 'Widdendream,' she proclaimed at tea, then clinked her teacup against her bedroom wall to seal the deal. She told me you laughed so happily, she never wanted your laughter to end."

"That was the greatest day of my life." Widdendream's soul pushed through the calm water, mists trailing it like a veil. "Right after your mother named me, the *W* appeared on my chest. I was happy, for many years. I had Mazarine, then Aubergine, and for a while, I had you and Celadon. But those days didn't last long."

Cecelia sighed and thought back on her life with Widdendream. How she got older and let it go. She never realized how much more she took than she gave, but she wouldn't make that mistake again.

"You and your brother got older, and often had better things to do than spend time with a broken-down house. Still," Widdendream continued with a half smile, "at least I had Mazarine. From the moment that girl came through my door, she always had time for me. To read to me, talk with me, or just sit in silence with me. She knew me better than anyone, and I knew her." It covered its face with its hands. "I loved her," it sobbed. "I loved all of you."

"Widdendream—"

"No. I don't want your pity." The broken spirit waded toward the windows. It gazed upward through the darkling seawater as if beholding a starry night sky. "Once you hear my confession about how your brother died, you won't *want* to pity me."

Oh souls. She'd been right. Widdendream *was* hiding something about Celadon's death. Cecelia gripped her pen tighter and shifted on her knees.

"The day before Celadon's fall, the winds blew so hard off the lake they whipped through the cracks in the attic walls and into the bars of my cage. My spirit grew feverish, my cage sick, and I shook with cold. Your mother sat in the attic with me for as long as she could, while you and Celadon fought in your room over paper dolls."

Cecelia nodded. "I remember." By the troubled look on the spirit's face, Cecelia knew what came next.

"After supper, you broke the banister, and offered to let me fix it. I jumped at the chance because you were right—I *liked* doing things for myself." It paced faster now, the twin fires in its eyes blazing. "So, sick or not, I agreed. Even though it's not what Mazarine wanted, *I* wanted to—for *me*! Getting older, everything starts falling apart. It's terrifying. Big things you have to let others repair for you. But until the spirit leaves the house and dies, fixing those small broken things keeps us alive, makes us feel like we still have worth."

The small greenish-yellowish soul faced Cecelia. It moved toward her, bathed inside her growing light. The tears around it swirled.

"After you and Celadon went to bed, I placed the banister knob on the top of the railing where it belonged, ready to fasten it, good as new. But at the same time, Mazarine approached the stairs. I couldn't let her see me fixing myself after she told you to do it." It flicked its eyes onto her. "I didn't want either of us to get in trouble, so I stopped what I was doing and told myself I'd come back for it later. Mazarine had been on her way to the attic to bring me a vase of daisies to cheer me up." Misty tears rolled down its cheeks and merged with the seawater below. "But, me being sick, they made me sneeze. Mazarine apologized and whisked them away to second floor, to the table at the top of the stairs. Time passed, and then . . ."

Cecelia gasped. "You fell asleep, too."

"Yes," it replied quietly. "Everyone did."

"I see."

"I woke a few hours later, shivering and coughing on dust. And, the light sleeper that he was, Celadon woke up, too." Widdendream sighed. "He didn't have a lot of time for me, what with his schoolwork and friends, but he did visit from time to time. So it wasn't unusual that he walked to the attic and"—Widdendream swallowed hard—"sat with me, hoping to make me feel better. And he did, for a time. Then, right before midnight, he started nodding off. I woke him and said, 'Time for bed, young man,' and like a good boy, he went."

Widdendream's spirit stared up at Cecelia like a lost child, chin shivering with regret. She lowered herself and met its gaze. "Go on, Widdendream, don't be afraid."

It blinked a few times and continued.

"Celadon, still groggy with sleep, headed to his room. I shook with fever but watched him go anyway to make sure he got back all right." Widdendream clenched its tiny fists and pushed them into its eyes. "He stopped to smell the daisies Mazarine put in the vase at the top of the stairs. At that exact moment, I got a chill and shuddered so violently, the vase and table shot forward, and Celadon fell back. The water from the daisies spilled and flowed down my crooked staircase. He grabbed onto the broken knob, but it didn't hold because I'd forgotten to come back and fix it, and Celadon . . . *slipped*."

Shuddering, Widdendream removed its fists from its eyes. When it looked at Cecelia, its sadness mirrored her own.

"Can you see why I hate myself? I was so distraught and scared I didn't know what to do. I couldn't stop coughing long enough to help him, not in my house form anyway, or my thrashing body might have hurt him even more. But if I left my cage to try and help, as the law of house spirits demands, I wouldn't be allowed back into my cage. And if I wasn't allowed back in, I'd have to leave. And if I told your parents what happened, they'd leave me. So I did nothing. I just . . . let him die."

Widdendream fell on its knees before her, lay its head in her lap, and cried. "I was so ashamed of what I'd done; it was easier just to blame you." It sobbed into her armor of daisies. Cecelia stroked its soft, trembling hand. "I never wanted to hurt anyone. But I thought if your family found out the truth, you'd all leave me. I couldn't bear being alone, Cecelia. I never could, but getting older made the loneliness worse. I was so afraid of dying alone. But now, after pushing my cage away, too, that's exactly what will happen." Its eyes beamed with soft golden light. "It's shameful how I treated you. And I don't expect your forgiveness. How could I, when I can't even forgive myself?"

Cecelia's tears floated on the water's surface like blue diamonds as she beheld the small sad thing. The light in its eyes tugged a memory from her mind by the roots.

"Widdendream, do you remember reading me a book called *The Wildflowers of Queen Morose*? In the story, moments before the heroine is put to death by an evil sorceress, she shouts to her crowd of tormentors, *'Love is like a wildflower: simple and abundant, able to grow in the most desolate places.'* The wicked crowd boos and mocks her, but she doesn't care. *'Ripped from the earth, wildflowers leave holes that store their memory. And always, from this emptiness, new wildflowers grow.'*"

Nodding, Widdendream answered with the ghost of a grin, "I remember reading you that story. You couldn't have been more than five years old."

"That's right. And then I asked you why the heroine would waste her last breaths telling those ignoramuses the truth about wildflowers—or love for that matter—when they'd all come to cheer while she died."

No longer green mist, Widdendream's body shimmered with pale lemon light. "And I replied: 'Life cannot grow without hope, and hope springs from a desire to love, and love and life always deserve a second chance.'"

"Yes." Cecelia regarded Widdendream with kindness. "Celadon's death was a tragedy. But not you, or I, or Father or Mother, or even Tuesday is to blame. That's something I've learned, Widdendream. All we can do is our best, learn from our mistakes and also from those we love. Then, when we're ready, we can finally move beyond Yesterday and return to living in Today."

Move beyond Yesterday and return to living in Today . . .
That's it.

Captain Shim's words whispered from memory: *"The only way to leave the Sea of Tears is to truly want to be in Today. Focus on where you wish to go, picture it clearly in your mind, and when you're ready to leave, trust the sea to show you the way."*

If she and Widdendream worked together, maybe they could return to Hungrig, house, parents, and all.

"Widdendream, we need to leave here—now."

The next second, the last remaining section of Cecelia's nonpapered skin prickled and pinched. She ran her fingers down the back of her neck to the patch of flesh at the top of her spine. Cecelia focused on the beat of the flesh-and-blood heart inside her parchment chest, and the fact that she wasn't all-the-way gone, and prepared to make her move.

"Cecelia?" the soul moaned in a sleepy voice. "I don't feel so well."

"Widdendream!" Cecelia ran to its side as it slipped to the floor. It appeared weak, dull, thin. One look at its fading spirit told her all she needed to know: soon it would die, and the house, and her parents trapped in its walls, would die with it.

They had run out of time.

Chapter 26

THE PEN REALLY IS MIGHTIER THAN THE SWORD

"Widdendream!" The withered spirit fell to the ground, soft and quiet as starlight. Cecelia scooped it up and sped across the room. She knelt before the part of the wall where her parents were taken in, and set Widdendream's soul beside her. "I have an idea about how to get us home, so stay with me, okay?"

Widdendream, more translucent each second, stared at the wall with remorse. "But how? Even if we could leave the sea and Yesterday, thanks to me, we'd have no house or family to go back to." It closed its large black eyes. "I would do anything to return to Today with our home and family intact. But that seems impossible now. . . ."

Cecelia regarded Widdendream's spirit gently, hesitantly, hopefully. When she spoke, it opened its eyes. "Sometimes the most impossible things are the things most worth fighting for. I'll tell you my plan, but first, I have to ask: Now that we understand each other a bit better, would you please release my parents from the wall?"

Widdendream shook its head. "I'm so weak. . . . I don't think I'm strong enough. Still, I suppose I could try?"

Cecelia's hair bounced around her shoulders and her lantern flared. "Yes, please."

"Very well." Widdendream reclosed its eyes. A moment later, the water blanketing the floors trembled. The wall where her parents were trapped shuddered. The baseboard shimmied and cracked. Then everything moving stilled.

Cecelia blinked at the wall expectantly, but Aubergine and Mazarine did not appear.

"I couldn't do it." Widdendream's soul, faded to barely a shadow, covered its face with its hands. "I'm so sorry."

Cecelia gulped back the fireball of emotion stuck in her throat. She took a few deep breaths and straightened her spine. "Well, we're still here, aren't we? And that means there's still hope. And if there's a hope of leaving Yesterday and returning to Today, we must keep trying. Mother, Father, and Celadon wouldn't want us to give up, would they?"

"No," Widdendream's spirit answered, mist rising from

its body like motes. "They'd want us to fight."

Cecelia grinned. "All right. Then we must—for them, and for us."

"For the Dahls," Widdendream replied with a bit more oomph.

"For all of us." Just then, Cecelia spotted something from the corner of her eye. Three perfectly cut paper dolls, no bigger than her hand, slipped free of the crack in the baseboard that Widdendream's soul had made and floated to the water's surface at once: an aubergine-colored one of her father, a mazarine-colored one of her mother, and a translucent one of celadon green for her ghost brother.

"Oh souls." Cecelia lifted her family gently and set one atop the other in her palm. "Widdendream, you were strong enough to let them go after all." She smiled through tears. "Thank you for giving their spirits back to me. Now I can carry them home, too."

Widdendream, almost invisible, looked away, ashamed. "Tell me your plan."

"Okay. I know it's not the same as having a cage of your own, but what if, just for now, I shelter you in my cage alongside our little family, as you did for us all these years? Maybe it would keep you alive and safe until we find you a new cage of your own."

Widdendream wheezed in a breath. "You are a kind and

clever girl, Cecelia. All this time, I always knew that." It rested its hand on hers. "Your idea just might work."

Cecelia grinned. "I was hoping you'd say that." With her free hand, and the generous help of her hair, Cecelia moved the vines covering her middle. The doors of herself opened at once, flooding the attic with light. To her surprise, Cecelia's cage was no longer rusted or broken, but pristine and new. The brass door unclicked and swung wide. "If you'll trust me, Widdendream," Cecelia said, holding out her hand, "this time, I promise to take good care of you."

The spirit, sheer as a golden haze, smiled gratefully up at her. "Thank you, I would like that very much."

Widdendream climbed onto Cecelia's hand and entered her cage. Once inside, the tiny spirit surged with warm yellow light. Grinning like a person-shaped sun, it leaned against her lamp, and lifted one hand in a not-quite goodbye. Widdendream sighed with contentment, made itself at home, and cried tears of joy.

"There," Cecelia said. "Now that you're safe, think about your wish to return to Today with our home and family intact. Focus on that wish with your whole heart, all right?" Widdendream's spirit nodded with eagerness.

Right away, the intoxicating scents of home met Cecelia's downturned face in a wisp of sweet familiarity: mountain winds blown in off the lake, Widdendream's library and beloved old books, her freshly washed blankets, green grass and daisies.

Home, she thought, and placed her lovely little family inside herself, alongside Widdendream's soul, cocooned in a dazzle of shine.

A rush of peace, unlike anything she'd ever felt, filled Cecelia so completely, her lantern glowed brighter than ever, even after she closed her doors.

Something Captain Shim said the first time they met rushed back to her: that only those who'd been sad enough to write letters with their unhappiest tears could turn into paper and see such miracles. That the real secret was remembering what made someone shine. Cecelia realized her answer right then.

Her family made her shine brightest of all.

I am their shelter now, she thought. *And it's up to me to protect them.*

All at once, songs of home and Hungrig, of lakes and fields, and of wind scented with blooms drifted toward her, calling her from downstairs.

Time to go, Cecelia thought, and hurried toward the door.

The moment she passed through the door frame, Cecelia raised her miraculous pen from her pocket, unscrewed the elaborate brass cap, and removed the corked inner canister of her saddest, most desolate tears. Cecelia took a deep breath, popped the cork, and let her tears go. They fell to the water at her feet in a pale-blue stream and blended with the tears of the world.

Cecelia had never felt so free.

In a slow dance of daisies and hair, Cecelia descended the staircase. And every joy and happiness her family had brought her whirled back in a flood: giggling with her mother over silly jokes nobody else would understand, heart-to-heart talks with her father as they worked on inventions side by side, the safety of being wrapped in their arms. She remembered the elation on Celadon's face whenever he'd asked her to play and she'd said yes—and, oh, it was the most beautiful smile. She recalled Widdendream singing "You Are My Sunshine" to her on cloudy days, and how good it always made her feel. At the same time, Cecelia remembered how strong she was. How she laughed from her belly, smiled at strangers, and treated animals with tender care. And she made sure to forgive herself, as she had forgiven everyone else. She remembered that she was good. That she loved her family eternally, and also, she loved herself.

Crossing the foyer in water that had risen up to her waist, Cecelia's joy was enormous, like a sunburst inside her heart.

By the time she had arrived at the front door, her always-want-to-remember memories grew so enormous, she cried tears of joy at all the love within her. No longer blue like before, Cecelia tears were bright and luminous, and spread through the sea like a wave. Beams of light shot through the water—as if the sun had fallen into the sea, as if her happy memories had cracked open the pit of the world and found only light at its core.

Then the seas fell quiet at once.

Focus on where you wish to go, picture it clearly in your mind, and when you're ready to leave, trust the sea to show you the way. . . .

"This will work," Cecelia said to her miraculously magical pen, which had filled itself with a phantasm of her happiest golden tears. "I believe, I believe, I believe." Cecelia put her pen back together, set it in her pocket, and raised her face to the ceiling, toward the surface of the sea. "Okay, Captain Shim, I'm ready to leave Yesterday and return to Today."

Captain Shim's voice echoed from somewhere above. "Farewell, Daughter of Paper and Tears. I always knew you'd find your answer. . . ."

Smiling, Cecelia closed her eyes.

She envisioned her home, back on their land in Hungrig, atop their lush green hill surrounded by grass and daisies. She imagined Widdendream restored to health and vigor, with a strong new cage, and fully functional burners. She pictured her mother and father as they were before this nightmare began, no longer paper dolls, back to their old happy selves. Cecelia had read that if someone died in Today, they couldn't return to the land of the living. Even still, she visualized her brother anyway, at peace and at home with them, no longer a paper doll. And finally, she imagined herself a flesh-and-blood, nonpaper girl, back home where she belonged.

The sunlight outside grew brighter, and then everything happened at once.

Cecelia's fingers prickled as if they were waking; when she held up her right hand, the tips of her fingers were no longer midnight blue but bronze, flesh, and real.

"Oh souls."

Next, the floors rumbled. The walls heaved. The bowels of the house shook.

"It's working!"

A beloved voice rang out just beyond the front door. *"III reeepaaay giiift . . . dryyyyy yooourrr teeears aaand heeeellp Ceceeeeliaaa baaack hoooommme."*

"Caterwaul?" Cecelia grabbed the handle of the front door as an evilly familiar thud, thud, THUD banged outside.

Her pulse ticked. Her mind tocked. More prickles on skin, more light, more thuds.

Three-fourths of a second later, the house lifted through the sea in a whoosh, into the starry night sky, and out the other side.

Chapter 27

THE BEGINNING AFTER THE END

The eerie white light of a full Hungrig moon flooded Cecelia's bedroom. Her clock read 12:01 a.m. Dark shadows slipped across her walls like rowboats on rough seas. Outside, wind tossed dead leaves past her window; branches scratched Widdendream's outer walls. The first thing Cecelia noticed was that she was shivering. Her clothes, the same ones she'd had on earlier—boots and all—were soaked, along with her hair. Like she'd taken a midnight swim in her clothes and forgotten.

The second thing she noticed was—

Thud.

Thud.

THUD.

Cecelia froze.

She'd thought she heard the same hair-raising noises moments ago, but these thuds were louder, closer.

Maybe she had imagined it?

Cecelia rolled over in bed. *Bed.* Why did it seem strange that she should be in bed? Cecelia contemplated going back to sleep until a soft but clear whimper floated into her room from downstairs.

She definitely heard that.

Cecelia noted the time again on her clock. Her pulse beat a symphony of blood: *I am awake just after midnight, the exact time Celadon fell.* Then she saw the date on her clock. It was the day her brother died. *I heard a thud and a whimper. Just like the first evil Tuesday . . .*

Maybe Celadon is still alive!

No time to waste, Cecelia threw off her covers. She leaped out of bed in such a hurry, she didn't notice her soaking wet rug, the puddles of tears dotting her floor, or the daisies peeking out from under her bedding. She failed to witness the four paper dolls at rest atop her sheets before they vanished in a glimmer of motes: one of mazarine, one of aubergine, one of translucent celadon green, and one of the sunniest lemon. She ignored the clatter of her miraculous pen as it plunged from bed to ground, and completely missed the note that slipped from the tube.

Dearest Cecelia,

The gift of yesterday is all I have to give. I did everything I could to guide your family back in time to when each Dahl was alive. But no matter how I tried to bring everyone back, the Law of yesterday and Today would not bend: once a body dies in Today, it is yesterday's to claim, and there is no bringing it back. I am sorry. I hope, no matter what happens today, this note finds you smiling.

Your friend beyond time,

The Caterwaul

P.S. yesterday doesn't like change, so things might be a bit . . . mixed up.

As Cecelia rushed across her room, she paid no mind to the fiery warmth blazing within her, or the light shining through her odd freckles like stars. It wasn't until real tears rolled down Cecelia's real cheeks that the truth finally sank in.

I was paper but now I'm real.

Throwing open her bedroom door, Cecelia found the hallway black as pitch. She thought of her mother. How when she left for the Land of Yesterday, the lights wouldn't work. Cecelia flipped on the lights. This time, they worked and shone brighter and sunnier than ever.

"Widdendream?" Cecelia raced across the hall.

"I'm here," Widdendream replied with a soft and urgent voice. "Please, Cecelia, *hurry*."

Happy Widdendream's soul was safe, Cecelia glanced at her parents' bedroom door—closed. Unlike Celadon's, which was flung wide. Waterlogged photographs, like those strewn about Widdendream's attic, glazed the dripping wet floors. Several other items—baby clothes, old letters, broken lamps, and a decrepit stuffed bear of Celadon's—lined the corridor, as if carried downstream from the attic. None of them were made of paper.

Another whimper erupted downstairs.

Heart in her throat, hair in a tizzy, Cecelia leaped over yesterday's treasures on her way to the staircase. Except when she looked downstairs, it wasn't her brother she found.

"Oh souls!" Aubergine and Mazarine Dahl lay perfectly still at the bottom of the stairs. Surrounded by attic debris, it was as if the house had spit their bodies out. She looked everywhere but couldn't see her brother.

As impossible as it seemed that her brother could be brought back to life, Cecelia had secretly hoped it was true.

She was sad, yet she let the sadness come. *No matter where I am, little brother,* she thought as she ran, *I am never far from you.*

Grabbing the banister knob on instinct, Cecelia hurled herself downstairs. It held steady, good as new.

In a pool of light and seawater tears, her parents rested, motionless. Cecelia knelt between them and shook them each gently in turn. "Mother, Father, wake up, we're home!" A giant welt ballooned on her mother's forehead. Cecelia's hair spilled over her shoulders to caress Mazarine's and Aubergine's cheeks. "Talk to me. Are you all right?"

Neither moved or made a sound. Their clothes and hair were saturated like hers, and their bodies, cold as ice.

Finally, her father sputtered, coughed, and opened his eyes.

Cecelia nearly burst with joy. "Father, you're okay!" Quickly, she rolled him onto his side. He coughed water until he was done. Cecelia did the same for her mother, hoping she'd cough, too.

Nothing happened at first. Cecelia stroked Mazarine's wet hair and cried hot, stinging tears, afraid she'd lose her. "Please, please, don't die."

Mazarine stiffened and choked, fighting for air. Her midnight-blue eyes popped wide; her gaunt cheeks flushed and colored with life as she inhaled a ferocious breath.

Cecelia grinned harder than she ever thought possible. "You're safe, both of you. You're real flesh-and-blood parents, and truly back home with me!"

Cecelia helped them into a sitting position. Her father blinked at Cecelia while wearing a slightly confused expression. Her mother hunched over and rubbed the welt on her forehead.

"We're fine, thanks to you." Mazarine gave her a sly grin. "Joan of Arc couldn't have done any better."

"She's right," Aubergine said, brushing damp hair from Cecelia's eyes. "I'm not sure how we got here exactly, but that lump on your mother's forehead definitely needs to get checked out." He shook his head; bits of soggy drywall plonked to the floor. "If you hadn't found us when you did, who knows what might have happened?"

Mazarine peered deeply into Cecelia's eyes. "Do you . . . have any idea how we got here?"

"I—" Cecelia glanced at her father, who seemed happier than he'd been in a long time. Smiling proudly, and bravely, Cecelia lifted her chin and proclaimed, "It appears you may have nearly drowned in tears, and almost certainly fell a long way down, but I heard you cry out, and came as fast as I could. You're safe, and here, and that's all that matters now."

The closer she inspected her parents, the realer everything

became. Her father, still dressed in the dark purple suit he wore earlier when he picked her up from school, had bits of shredded paper sticking out of the collar. His skin bore a countless number of paper cuts. Daisy petals and seaweed poked from her mother's dress pockets and boots, the same clothes she'd been wearing in Yesterday. Plus, Cecelia could've sworn that when she knelt at her parents' sides, she heard a door creak inside herself.

Curiously, neither parent commented on the strangeness of these events.

"Well," Mazarine said to her daughter, wearing a shining smile worth every one of Cecelia's terrible yesterdays, "thank goodness you heard us, because I am a bit dizzy, and seeing a doctor is probably a good idea."

Aubergine and Cecelia helped Mazarine to her feet.

"Yes indeed," her father replied with a special twinkle in his eye—the twinkle of sharing a secret. "You saved us, Cecelia. Our daughter is a hero, Maz, don't you think?"

Mazarine hugged Cecelia fiercely. "That's right, a true hero. And I couldn't be more proud."

A flash of light from the windows at the front of the house stole Cecelia's attention. They crinkled and shone like smiling eyes. The air warmed, and the walls glowed in that same pale-yellow light.

Widdendream seemed happy at last.

"Okay, love," Aubergine said quietly to Mazarine while escorting her to the door. "Let's get you to the hospital. Cecelia, you might want to grab a sweater. It seems a bit wet out tonight."

Cecelia smirked. "It does seem especially damp everywhere. How curious."

When her father opened the front door, a warm breeze poured inside. Night clouds danced across the heavens. Crickets chirped. The Dahls' front yard bloomed with a fresh batch of daisies. The whole outdoors glistened with moonlit dew. Widdendream stood strong and fixed, shiny and pristine. The wrought-iron lantern alongside the walkway glowed more radiant than ever. So bright, in fact, the lone lantern illuminated not only their street, but the entire hill. Like a spotlight to the stars. Miraculously enough, the eyes of each Dahl glittered with that same fiery light.

As grateful as Cecelia was to be home and to have her parents back at her side, she couldn't help wishing her brother were here with them, too.

They got in the car and drove. Gazing out the window from the back seat, Cecelia noticed a giant housecat crossing their lawn. It looked suspiciously like a miniature Caterwaul, and winked at her as it passed.

She winked at it right back.

Suddenly, a pale-green shiver of light appeared at Cecelia's side.

Her heart stopped. Her hair rose. Her eyes danced with joy as they settled on Celadon's ghost. He was so faint she could barely see him, but he was here, and he was smiling.

"Celadon," she whispered. "You came back."

"If you hadn't carried me out of the Land of Yesterday," he spoke in near silence, as if calling from one mountain over, "I'd have stayed paper for eternity. You saved me, Cee-Cee, like you saved them." He patted the space over his misty heart. "Thank you, big sister. Don't forget, wherever I am, I'm never far from you."

Cecelia glanced at her parents in the front seat. They talked quietly to each other yet peered back more often than usual. She wondered briefly if they sensed him here, too. "Will you stay here, with us?"

Celadon didn't answer, too preoccupied in observing the sky. Cecelia followed his line of vision. Against a backdrop of silver night clouds, a rainbow-striped hot-air balloon drifted in and out of sight. Cecelia waved as it passed by.

"Today is a good day," Celadon replied at last, his voice soft as falling snow. "Don't you think?"

"Today is brilliant," Cecelia whispered back as he blinked out of sight.

Their parents cracked the windows. The scents of dampness and drying tears and Hungrig drifted around them. Together, Aubergine, Mazarine, and Cecelia inhaled deeply of the cool mountain air. The kind of breath you take to make sure you're alive.

ACKNOWLEDGMENTS

Hello, dear reader. I am so glad you're here because before I acknowledge the many incredible people who helped bring this book to life, I want to thank you for reading (thank you so much!) and tell you a secret: the true story of how Cecelia's story began many years ago with another girl who lost her mother to the Land of Yesterday, and the very real letter that started it all.

My mother died suddenly when I was seven years old. After I found out, I went into the basement and wrote her a letter asking her why she left me and if she was coming back. I stuffed the note into an envelope I made myself, stood in the center of the room, and closed my eyes. A seven-year-old's logic assured me that if I threw my letter into the air, my mother would catch it in heaven. She'd see how much I missed her and come home. But when I threw my note high, it hit the ceiling and floated back down unread. I remember falling to my knees in tears and burying my face in the carpet with the realization that she was never coming back. The memory of those tears and that letter stayed with me all this time. And though I don't remember what happened to that letter, I'd like to think it found its way into my heart for safekeeping. For the day I was finally ready to write this book.

Now, without further ado, let the festival of thanks begin!

Endless thanks to my brilliant superhero agent, Thao Le, for loving this story from the beginning. You saw the heart of this book and worked with me through several revisions to help make it really shine. Every step of the way you were kind and generous and amazing, and each suggestion you made was right. Not only did you answer my million questions, but you found this book the perfect home. My dream truly began with you.

So much gratitude to my kind and ingenious editor, Emilia Rhodes. I am eternally grateful that you saw something special in Cecelia's story and knew just what needed to happen to make it even better. You could not be a lovelier human. Thank you with my whole heart for bringing my dream to life. I'd also love to thank the entire Harper team for championing this book. You've all helped make my dream come true.

Eternal glory to Helen Musselwhite for creating the stunningly unique work of art that is the cover of this book. She truly brought Cecelia and the atmosphere of her world to life. I cried when I saw Cecelia's face. Thank you for those happy, happy tears. Also, many thanks to Jensine Eckwall for the spectacular internal illustrations. They couldn't be more perfect.

A ginormous thank-you to my incomparable, all-powerful, superlative critique partners given to this earth by the gods. This book would be nowhere without you:

First, to the exquisite Jennifer Hawkins. My friend and soul sister, there are not enough words or orange Starbursts in the world to thank you for all you've done for me. You kept me going when I wanted to quit. You reminded me to believe when my belief had run dry. You sent me inappropriate GIFs when I needed them most. Without your encouragement, humor, praise, and love, I would have quit years ago. Like I always say, I love you, Jennifer Hawkins!

To Jaye Robin Brown, the first reader of this story, and Kim Graff and Sonia Hartl: without your constant insights, brilliance, and excitement, this book would not exist, and I wouldn't be the writer I am today. I treasure you. Love and thanks also to April Rose Carter, Kristin Thorsness, Destiny Vandeput, Breeana Shields, Kari Mahara, Kip Rechea, P. J. Sheridan, Ron Walters, those who had eyes on this book in contests and helped me shape the first pages, and anyone else that my head-in-the-clouds brain may have forgotten. You each added something special to this story, and I'll always be grateful for that.

Thank you to my writers group, Querying Authors, and to my people, the 2014 Pitch Wars Mentees. My god, you guys, without you I'd have shriveled up into a husk from so many spent writer's tears and eventually would have blown away in a sad, sad wind. You kept me sane during every Dark Night of the Soul. Heartfelt thanks to each of you for your friendship, faith, and unwavering support. And finally, a big group hug of gratitude to the Electric Eighteens, the most eclectic and seriously talented group of debuts ever!

To Brenda Drake and Pitch Wars for giving me my mentors, the 2014's, and Pit Mad, the contest where I found my amazing agent. You've done so much for so many, thank you.

Lastly, eternal praises, love, and thanks to my family: the hearts that beat alongside my heart. Goodness, here come the tears. Breathe, Kristin, breathe!

To my mother, who showed me the true meaning of bravery and how deeply one can love. Not a day goes by that I am not missing you. To my grandmother, the quiet warrior who saved me in every way one can be saved and who, by some divine miracle, never gave up on me: thank you for loving me anyway. To Hugh and Mark, my uncles, my brothers, thank you for always being there for me, you big goofy things, I love and cherish you more than you know. To Alex, thank you for your continuous love, generosity, and support.

To Bob, who always believed in my dream, even when it seemed impossible. I love you for that and so much more. Thank you (so many miles). And to the epitome of my life's work, my strange and wonderful children, Michael, Jonah, Liam, Ava, and Indy, who light me up when my fires go out. I love you more than words, and there is no monster in any world I wouldn't fight to get to you.

To Cecelia, the friend I needed as a child and found as an adult, thank you for finding me at just the right time—on my knees, ready to give up writing forever, and for holding my hand in the dark and showing me the way.

Finally, thank you to grief, the root from which this book was born. You taught me pens are magic. Light is born from darkness. Tears are powerful. And, perhaps most important, you showed me that love is like a wildflower, simple and abundant, able to grow in the most desolate places, and that even when they're ripped from the earth, they leave holes that hold their memory and always, from this emptiness, new wildflowers grow.

Thank you all from the depths of my own wild heart.